"Goodbye, Miss Carstairs. See You in Class."

She found her voice. "Goodbye, Professor Hanson." Turning away from the desk, she made her way blindly past the next student and down the hall. This was even worse than she had expected it to be.

Mark Hanson had not lost his appeal for her. If anything, the years had made him even more attractive. And every time she looked at him, old memories surfaced, memories of kisses and touches and lovemaking. Memories that should have been obliterated forever. . . .

NORA POWERS

taught English at the college level while working on her Ph.D. A prolific writer, she is the author of some 500 pieces of children's verse, 58 short stories, 24 novels, and various newspaper articles. She has been a published author for the last twenty years and reports, "I don't even recall how I started writing, I was so young."

Dear Reader:

SILHOUETTE DESIRE is an exciting new line of contemporary romances from Silhouette Books. During the past year, many Silhouette readers have written in telling us what other types of stories they'd like to read from Silhouette, and we've kept these comments and suggestions in mind in developing SILHOUETTE DESIRE.

DESIREs feature all of the elements you like to see in a romance, plus a more sensual, provocative story. So if you want to experience all the excitement, passion and joy of falling in love, then SILHOUETTE DESIRE is for you.

Karen Solem
Editor-in-Chief
Silhouette Books

NORA POWERS
This Brief Interlude

Silhouette Desire
Published by Silhouette Books New York
America's Publisher of Contemporary Romance

SILHOUETTE BOOKS, a Division of Simon & Schuster, Inc.
1230 Avenue of the Americas, New York, N.Y. 10020

ISBN: 0-671-47204-6

First Silhouette Books printing February, 1984

10 9 8 7 6 5 4 3 2 1

America's Publisher of Contemporary Romance

Printed in the U.S.A.

BC91

For Ruth Ann and Margaret
with thanks for their friendship

1

The CSU cafeteria walls echoed with the clatter of silverware against dishes, the rise and fall of many student voices. At a coveted table by one of the large windows, Claudia Carstairs looked out over the city of Cleveland. The view—buildings of weathered brick and old houses beyond the new parking garage—had its own kind of charm. But Claudia was oblivious to everything but her problem.

She ran a nervous hand through her shoulder-length blond hair and stared unseeing into her Styrofoam cup. How could this have happened to her? She had kept her life within such orderly boundaries—except for that one disastrous night. And now that night had come back to haunt her.

Her coffee grew cold and the babble of voices around her faded as her mind slipped back in time.

She couldn't really be blamed, said one part of her mind. After all, she'd only been eighteen. And Mark Hanson had been eight years older. So handsome, so attractive.

It hadn't just been his uniform, either, or some kind of misplaced patriotism. Her family, like many other university-oriented people, had opposed the U.S. intervention in Vietnam. It had been Mark Hanson himself—the dark, handsome boy next door grown into a man. A man that she had worshiped from afar for so many years.

At eighteen, and left in charge of the house for the first time when her parents were called away because of her aunt's death, she had felt very adult. Out in the backyard sunbathing and reviewing her duties, she heard a long low whistle come floating over the fence. She sat up, startled by such a sound coming from the Hansons' backyard, especially as she had thought their son was overseas.

Turning, she met the gaze of a pair of warm brown eyes. Mark Hanson's eyes. Her whole body flushed—and there was a lot of it exposed in that bikini—but she wasn't going to appear even more foolish by grabbing for her towel.

"Hello there!" He was wearing civilian clothes, light slacks and a pale blue shirt. She hadn't seen him for four years, but he didn't look much older, this man who had haunted her dreams ever since she could remember.

"Hello," she replied, trying to act like the flip girls at school and not the tongue-tied idiot she usually felt with boys she liked.

"I didn't know the Carstairs family had moved,"

Mark said, his mouth stretching in a wide grin, his eyes appraising.

"They haven't." She forced herself to meet his eyes. "I'm Claudia Carstairs."

"Claudia!" His eyes were frankly admiring. "You mean you're that skinny little kid?"

"Afraid so." She was enjoying this talk, she discovered.

"Boy, have you changed!"

"You look a lot the same," she ventured. "A little older, maybe."

His grin didn't falter. "I am a little older. Say, are you busy tonight? I mean, I know it's Friday and kind of late in the day. But I didn't know you were there. Maybe we could have dinner? Go to a movie or something?"

She pretended to be considering this, while her heart pounded in her throat. As if she would ever say no to Mark Hanson! "Yes, I think that could be arranged."

"Great. See you around seven."

And that had been the beginning. She laced her fingers together and regarded them absently. The beginning of the most wonderful weekend of her life. For they had spent the evening together, and the next day, and had dinner *that* evening, too. And after dinner, heady with the triumph of being with him, of being treated like an adult, of realizing the dream of so many years, she responded to his kisses with an ardor that had surprised even her. The kisses led to other things and eventually to her first time with a man, though she managed to hide that fact from him.

Crimson flooded her cheeks now; after twelve long

years, the thought of that night still made her flush. It hadn't seemed like a mistake then. The realization of her mistake had come later, when the weeks passed and no letters arrived from Vietnam.

In the meantime, the boys at school had lost their appeal. They seemed different: dull, juvenile. Nothing to compare to Mark.

She was finally forced to the inevitable conclusion that the night that had seemed out of this world to her had been nothing so unusual for Mark. Not even worth a single letter.

But by that time she had decided on her career and she had no time for men. She was going to be as good a drama scholar as her father was a Shakespearian one. And that took up most of her energies.

Claudia sighed. She had survived the news of Mark's marriage to a Vietnamese girl and the subsequent announcement of the arrival of his child, both so innocently passed on by her mother, who knew nothing of what had transpired on that fateful weekend. But she didn't know how she was going to handle *this*.

She yearned to go hide in a dark corner and give way to her feelings. But she had an appointment in half an hour, and the office she shared with other graduate students was almost as noisy as the cafeteria. She had to face the facts. Mark Hanson was back in her life again.

Now an acknowledged scholar in the field of Asian drama and a full professor at thirty-eight, he was in Cleveland preparing to lead a special summer session on a tour of Southeast Asia, where they would study native forms of drama.

Claudia's knowledge of such theater was minimal.

She knew the English theater backward and forward, from its beginnings down to the nineteenth century. Her dissertation was to be on the performances of the great English actor Edmund Kean. But it was precisely for that reason that her beloved father had given her this summer session as a gift.

"Get away for a while," he said. "Forget about Shakespeare. There are other forms of drama, you know." To her objection that she had no time to study such nonessentials, he had replied, "You've been working too hard, Claudia. That's why I put you down to audit. Just observe. Relax. Have a good time."

His face, usually so serious, had taken on a strange expression. "You're still a young woman, Claudia. Live a little. Your dissertation will go that much faster for your having had a rest and some fun. Believe me, I know."

She had wracked her brain to find a reason for not going that he would find acceptable, but she could come up with nothing. Nothing except the truth, and she couldn't bring herself to divulge that foolishness. So she was condemned to taking this trip, to spending all that time in close proximity to Mark Hanson.

She had not seen him since that weekend so long ago. She'd managed to be away the first time he came home to visit, bringing his Vietnamese family. And then the Hansons had moved to Florida. Maybe he had grown fat and bald, she told herself in a futile attempt to raise her spirits. But, somehow, she could not see Mark letting himself go. He had always been . . .

Her mind presented her with a series of pictures: Mark at eighteen playing ball in his backyard; at twenty, roaring out of the drive in his car; at twenty-six, in his uniform. And in the darkness of the motel room where he had taken her, his lean brown body glowing in the reflection of the neon lights.

The first man's body she had ever seen. And the last. For the pain that had followed his departure had been almost too much to bear. As the days grew into weeks and the weeks into months and still there was no word, she had vowed never to expose herself to such agony again. She had managed to bury the pain, bury it so deep that it was forgotten forever. Or so she had thought until her father had sprung this surprise on her.

With a sigh, she drank the last of her coffee, now cold and bitter, and glanced at her watch. In a few minutes she was due in Mark Hanson's office for her orientation interview. And it was the last place on this earth that she wanted to be. She pushed back her chair. Nevertheless, she would be there. The Carstairses did not ignore appointments, most especially the academic kind.

As she made her way down the stairs and through the center of the five-story building whose glass and concrete walls had earned it the nickname of "The Cage," she tried to think of what she would say to Mark Hanson. Certainly none of the things she was thinking. She would not ask him why there had been no letters, no word, after that wonderful weekend. She would not even *think* of that weekend. He had forgotten it. So would she.

She crossed the concrete plaza that separated The Cage from the tower that housed the English department, the department where Mark Hanson had been given an office. The air was cool, the sunshine warm, but it might as well have been blizzarding for all she noticed. She took the elevator to the eighteenth floor. Her knees were trembling as she stepped out, and she cursed silently under her breath. She was not going to walk into Mark Hanson's office quivering like some terrified freshman. She was thirty years old, a graduate student of acknowledged ability. And she was going to act like it.

She took a deep breath and rounded the corner. The door was slightly ajar; she knocked tentatively.

"Come in."

His voice was even deeper than she remembered it, and gooseflesh rose on her arms. Her mouth went suddenly dry. Never in her life had she been so tempted to turn tail and run. She took another deep breath and forced herself to push open the door and take the few steps that would bring her inside.

He was looking at the door, face expectant. She managed to return his welcoming smile.

"Claudia Carstairs," he said, glancing down at the folder on his desk.

"Yes."

"Come in, Claudia. Sit down."

She was thankful for the chair. Her legs were very unsteady. She settled into it and made herself look across the desk at him.

He looked older, of course, but he was neither fat nor bald. His hair was longer than she remembered it, with a little gray at the temples, but his body seemed as lean and athletic as ever. Certainly he was just as attractive. The old feelings of longing, feelings she had thought buried forever, rose up in great waves. To her dismay she realized that she wanted desperately to touch him.

"So you're a drama major now."

15

"Yes, English drama. My main area is early nineteenth century, but I'm familiar with what came before."

He smiled. "Since you're Professor Carstairs's daughter, I'm sure you are. How are your parents?"

"My father retired last year. Mother's been gone two years now. She was ill for some time. That's why my schooling was delayed."

She swallowed hastily, steeling herself for the return query that courtesy dictated. "And how is your family? Your wife and child?"

His face went blank, all emotion wiped away. "My parents are doing well. They like Florida. My wife and child were killed. In an auto accident. A year ago this August."

"I . . . I'm sorry. After your folks moved away we lost touch." So much for politeness, she thought bitterly.

"That's all right." His tone was noncommittal, but his eyes could not quite hide his pain. "I'm getting used to it. It just takes a while to get over the loss of those you love. But I'm sure you know that."

She nodded. Yes, she knew. She knew very well. Hadn't she lost him? And had to manage her grief without the aid of others? Do her crying in secret?

He shook himself as though putting the subject behind him. "So you're a drama major. What made you decide to study Asian drama?"

"I didn't really decide to," she explained. "I know next to nothing about it." She shrugged. "As far as I'm concerned, drama *is* Shakespeare, and the golden age began with Garrick and ended with Kean. Anything else is second-best. Definitely inferior."

If she had hoped to irritate him—and she knew that she had—she saw that she had failed. He did not rise to her bait.

"A wonderful period. And two tremendous, though vastly different, performers. I suppose you'll be dealing with the controversy of Nature versus Art, Kean versus Kemble."

"Yes. My dissertation is on Kean." So, he knew more than just Asian theater.

"Sounds interesting. So why are you going on this tour?"

"My father gave it to me as a gift." She couldn't help it if she didn't sound suitably grateful. "To be frank with you, I'd rather stay here and work on my dissertation. But he seems to think I need a rest. So he paid my tuition for this class, and signed me up just to audit so I can do as much or as little as I please."

"I see." He spread his hands in a gesture of resignation. "It doesn't take much insight to tell that you aren't exactly enthusiastic."

She nodded. There was a certain grim satisfaction in laying her feelings about this on the line. At least she could be honest about this thing. "I'm quite convinced that Shakespearian drama is the greatest ever written, and Edmund Kean its greatest actor. But my father wants me to take this trip. And it won't take all that much time away from my work."

"Well, Claudia, I can only hope that this tour will help you change your mind. The East is a fascinating place. Very different, of course. But intriguing. I think you'll find the trip more enjoyable than you now believe."

She did not answer this. At that moment she could

only think of how uncomfortable being so close to him made her. Little things she had thought long forgotten were surfacing now. The sight of his dark slender hands, which he used so effectively when he gestured, was waking memories of his touch, memories that she didn't want or need. This man had betrayed her once, she reminded herself harshly. Used her and left her in the age-old way of soldiers on leave. He might be so attractive that he made her breath catch in her throat and her heart pound. He might know everything there was to know about Asian drama—or even about Shakespeare and Kean. But books and knowledge were one thing, character another. And she knew things about Mark Hanson's character that no sensible woman could afford to ignore.

"Well," he said, glancing down at his watch. "It was good talking to you."

She was grateful he didn't try to smile with this obviously polite lie. For though his features were unruffled and his voice calm, she sensed that her responses had troubled him. Well, let them, she thought bitterly. She was no longer a starry-eyed virgin, hanging on his every word.

"I am sorry you're not looking forward to our tour," he continued. "There's a wealth of knowledge in this area, and Western scholarship has practically ignored it. It's time we Americans looked beyond our Anglo-European heritage and discovered a little more of the world."

She was tempted to tell him sharply that she was quite satisfied with her heritage, but common sense stopped her. That, and the fact that in principle she agreed with him. In today's world no one could afford to remain insular.

"Well, I suppose you have all the material the department sent out?"

"Yes."

"And your passport?"

"Yes."

"You've seen the doctor about your inoculations?"

"Tomorrow," she replied.

"Well, then, it looks like you're all set." He pushed back his chair and got to his feet. "I'll see you at the orientation lecture next Monday. You will be there?"

"Of course." Since she was accepting this gift from her father, she would attend all the events. He would want to know about everything when she returned. She was sure of that.

She got to her feet as she spoke. It was then that she saw his outstretched hand. Panic assailed her. She couldn't touch him; she just couldn't. But she couldn't pretend not to see the gesture. It was too late for that. And to ignore it would be really insulting.

She swallowed over the sudden lump in her throat and reached across the desk to put her hand in his. She meant to make the handshake minimal, a quick gesture. But his fingers closed around hers tightly— warm, strong fingers whose touch flooded her whole body with longing.

His eyes, their dark warm brown intense, found hers and held them. "I really am glad to see you again, Claudia. And I hope you'll give the tour—and me—a chance to prove ourselves."

She didn't trust herself to speak—not with that lump in her throat and his hand still enfolding hers. A terrible urge to step into his arms came rushing over her and she was grateful for the desk that separated them.

A knock sounded on the door, interrupting the moment. Mark released her hand. "Just a minute," he called. "Goodbye, Miss Carstairs. See you in class."

She found her voice. "Goodbye, Professor Hanson." Turning away from the desk, she made her way blindly past the next student and down the hall. This was even worse than she had expected it to be.

Mark Hanson had not lost his appeal for her. If anything, the years had made him even more attractive. And every time she looked at him, old memories surfaced, memories of kisses and touches and lovemaking. Memories that should have been obliterated forever.

2

Her face set almost grimly, Claudia took a seat in the last row of the small classroom and opened her notebook. The week that had elapsed since that meeting in Mark Hanson's office had not made her any more satisfied with the idea of this trip. In fact, her every waking moment, and many of her sleeping ones, had been haunted by Mark's darkly handsome face. Every second of their weekend together had been run and rerun through her mind. Like a video playback that had gone berserk, it played and replayed every scene until she felt like screaming.

Now she wished for a bigger classroom, a larger group of students. Either would provide more of a buffer between her and Mark. But there were only ten students making the trip. In such a small number of people she would inevitably be thrown into close contact with Mark.

She sighed and fished out her pen. Maybe if she concentrated on the subject matter, on what he was saying instead of on the man.

"Hi, Claudia."

She looked up as Dell Edwards slipped into the seat beside her. Fair-haired and blue-eyed, Dell hardly looked his thirty years. And often he didn't act it. "Hello, Dell. What are you doing here?"

"Same as you." He grinned engagingly. "I'm off to see the wonders of Asian theater. I finally managed to squeeze a little loan out of the old man."

Claudia suppressed a smile. Reluctant to leave her widowed father alone in the big house in Cleveland Heights, she still lived at home, so she felt she hadn't much room to criticize. But, after all, she was a responsible member of the family, and during her mother's protracted illness, living elsewhere had been out of the question.

Dell didn't live at home, of course. It hampered his freedom, as he had jokingly explained more than once. But he was never averse to "hitting up" his father for extra money. And he did it—successfully, too—with a frequency that rather astonished Claudia, accustomed as she was to a one-salary, academic family's rather frugal style of living.

"So you're interested in Asian drama," she said, more to make conversation than anything else. She had known Dell from childhood, before his father had attained the wealth that had made him so easy to "hit up," and she was accustomed to his easy attitude toward life.

"What I'm interested in is getting away from Cleveland for a while," he replied cheerfully. "The old man is a sucker for anything educational or cultural. So I'm off to see the world."

Claudia shook her head. "This is a class, you know. You'll have to do some work."

He shrugged. "I'll manage. There'll still be plenty of time for fun." He leaned toward her suggestively. "Speaking of which, want to share a room?"

This was not the first time Dell had laughingly suggested that they get together. Nor would it be the last, since she was aware that he was at least half-serious. She shook her head. "Sorry, Dell. My father put me down as a single."

He grinned. "OK then, I'll share *your*—" he began.

A stirring among the students turned all heads toward the door. Mark Hanson entered, pulling the door shut behind him. "Hello, class," he said. "I suppose you're all eager to get down to business."

He moved toward the blackboard, letting his eyes rove over the group. They seemed to linger a long time on her face, and Claudia struggled not to blush.

"I believe everyone is here," he continued. "I assume you've all received your information sheets. You've got your passports." He paused. "Your inoculations." A general groan went up from the group. He smiled. "The shots are much less painful than the diseases they prevent. I can assure you of that."

He looked around the room. "Now, the tour will begin in Singapore. Then we'll be stopping at Bangkok, Rangoon, Jakarta and Bali, then back to Singapore. We'll be spending roughly two days in each place. One day there will be a lecture and some kind of local drama to observe. The other day you'll be more or less on your own.

"There's a great deal to see. If you should choose to spend your free day further investigating drama, there'll be plenty of material available. Remember, your grade depends on your paper and it's due the Monday before fall quarter begins."

He chuckled. "The paper needn't be book length. I'm after quality, not quantity. Fifteen or twenty pages will do. But it should be intelligent, original, and based on what you have observed. No rehashes out of books, please."

He looked around the classroom once more. "Now, I want to give you a little general information. You'll get more specifics in the individual lectures as we move from place to place."

Claudia couldn't help it. Looking at his face brought back those old memories. Yet where else could she look? After all, this was a class.

"First," Mark continued, "you must not think of this theater as another kind of Western drama. It's very different. Now, say we were discussing the American theater. Which kind of play would rank higher, be considered more 'serious'—*Death of a Salesman* or *The King and I?*"

A subdued giggle ran around the room.

Mark nodded. "Of course. Everyone knows that tragedy is the highest ranking form of drama. Serious. Artistic."

Heads nodded. Claudia's too. She was trying to listen, to get the sense of the words as well as the sound of his voice. But she was finding it difficult. Especially since no matter where he looked, his eyes seemed to be focusing right on her.

"In America," he continued, "we rate musicals very low. We call them musical comedies even though many of them embody serious ideas. Can someone name me such a musical?"

"Cabaret," came one answer.

"Camelot," Claudia said softly.

Mark's eyes came back to her and seemed to soften momentarily. "Very good. Now, if you'll think about these—and I'm sure others will come to mind, even our first example, *The King and I*—you'll see that they have music, comedy, *and* serious thought. What we call a message."

He paused. "Serious Western drama, particularly in its later developments, does not include music, and often has little or no humor. Although Shakespeare" —his gaze sought Claudia again—"knew the value of a little humor even in the darkest of tragedies. Take the gravedigger scene in Hamlet, for instance."

Claudia found herself nodding. He knew his drama; there was no denying that.

"The theater we are going to be seeing doesn't make such distinctions. We have a tendency to compartmentalize life. The Asians go the other way. Their drama, even their most serious drama, includes music and comedy. Division into categories, such as those of the Greek comedy and tragedy, does not make much sense to Asians. To a degree, they are a fatalistic people. A hero like Oedipus, who struggles against the fate decreed for him by the gods, is not heroic in their eyes. He's just a fool. An idiot. Heroism lies in fighting evil, not in a useless battle against one's destiny."

Claudia tried to digest this. It was certainly a very different way to consider drama. How could anything be better than Shakespeare? Or even as good?

He looked around the room. "I don't expect you all to come back Asian experts," he said. "What I do expect from each and every one of you"—this time it seemed he deliberately *didn't* look at her—"is an open mind. Give this theater a chance, peculiar as it may seem to you, and you'll discover its fascination.

"I expect that you are accustomed to thinking of theater in terms of living people, actors and actresses."

Heads nodded in agreement.

"The theater we are going to study is quite varied. You'll have the chance to see shadow plays, folk rituals, spirit dances, classic Chinese opera, even puppet plays. Plays may be based on subjects as divergent as the Buddhist Jataka stories, the Mahabharata and Ramayana cycles, and the works of Shakespeare or Oscar Wilde. I'm not sure that we will come upon any of the latter. But if we do, I should warn you that such adaptations may seem strange to you. Characters not in the original may be added for romantic interest or other reasons."

"Like when a novel gets made into a movie," someone volunteered.

"Exactly," Mark said. "But, varied as the forms are, they are closely related. Coming from similar cultural settings, they share certain elements."

He ran a hand through his hair. "You must understand that our trip will only allow us to see a small number of performances. I've tried to arrange the tour so you can experience a variety of forms."

He indicated the table where he had put a stack of papers. "This is a glossary, a list of forms of drama. Read it over. Try to familiarize yourself with the terms. You'll find the definitions quite straightforward. I have not assigned a text for the course. The emphasis here is on experience. You may never have a chance to see such performances again. The world changes rapidly these days. The spread of Western technology—you'll note I don't refer to it as progress or civilization—"

The class laughed.

"Anyway, with the subsequent advance of mass media forms of entertainment, the existence of many of the old forms grows precarious. This is inevitable, of course, especially in a theater with such a large basis in folk ritual."

He stepped toward the desk. "That's it for today. I'll see you Friday morning at eight by the tower door in the parking lot. The minibus will take us from there to the airport. Are there any questions?" His eyes surveyed the room once more. Claudia felt their pressure as a tangible physical touch before they moved on.

Dell raised his hand. "Our whole grade is based on the paper? There are no exams, no orals or anything?"

A flitting expression of distaste marred Mark's handsome features for the briefest moment. "It goes without saying, Mr. Edwards, that I expect all students to attend the briefing lectures and scheduled performances. As I've already pointed out, the free days can be used as you see fit. I would expect a genuine scholar to take advantage of such an educational opportunity."

His voice was correct, with no overt sarcasm, yet Claudia understood the implication that Mark was not at all sure about the quality of Dell's scholarship.

"Since we are all adults in this room," continued Mark, "I do not intend to call each of you in and give you a grilling. There will be ample opportunity for discussion and I will be glad to answer any and all questions. But I don't intend to force anyone's participation."

Again Claudia felt he was avoiding looking her way. She was almost as uncomfortable as if he had been.

"If it were up to me, I wouldn't assign grades at all," Mark went on. "But the educational process, faulty as it is, has to be served. So I have asked you for a paper."

His voice softened. "It's really very simple. I love this theater in all its varied and complex forms. I want to share it with you."

There was silence in the room as the students absorbed this. Then, one by one, they rose and went forward to get their handouts.

Claudia, reluctant to face his eyes alone, turned toward Dell. Should she attach herself to him? She really didn't want to encourage him. Dell could make a nuisance of himself, given half a chance.

She suppressed a sigh and got to her feet. She would just pick up her handout and walk out. There was no need for anything more. And to her surprise that was exactly what she did.

The days passed far too quickly for Claudia, and Friday morning found her with butterflies in her stomach and an iron determination to avoid Mark Hanson as much as possible.

In the minibus, she managed to squeeze in between Dell and another woman student. As they boarded the jet and she took a seat, her heart was in her throat. In spite of all her precautions, several times she had turned and found Mark's eyes on her. If he decided to sit by her . . .

"Hi." It was Dell again, wearing his inevitable grin. "Saving this seat for someone?" he inquired cheerfully. "For me, maybe?"

Claudia shook her head. "No. Not for anyone."

"Then I'll just take it." And he stuffed his coat in the overhead rack and dropped down beside her.

She leaned her head back against the seat, the action automatically causing her eyes to look ahead up the aisle. And there he was, coming toward her. For a moment, her heart jumped up in her throat and her whole body was suffused with warmth. She knew she should pull her eyes away; she did not want to get caught looking at him. But there was something about the slant of his head, the curve of his shoulder, the way his hair lay against his coat collar, that brought back a vivid memory of the younger man and the love she had felt for him.

He turned toward her suddenly and their eyes met. The contact between them was very brief—so brief she was sure no one else saw it. But her nerve endings felt scorched from its intensity. He might as well have touched her.

She dropped her eyes to her lap as he passed her seat. If only her body would stop this insane remembering. It was affecting her perceptions of everything. Certainly nothing Mark Hanson had said or done had indicated any wish on his part to renew their intimacy. He seemed to have erased it from his mind. She only wished she could do so as easily, could stop being haunted by those memories and feelings which seemed to grow stronger with every glimpse of him.

Each look, each gesture, brought back another memory, usually one fraught with emotion. For in spite of the pain that accompanied them, she had never succeeded in eradicating the memories of those wonderful hours in his arms.

She took her guidebook out of her purse and tried

to focus her attention on it. She had decided to come on this trip; she would just make the best of it. Anything could be borne for a while. After all, the trip would last less than two weeks. Then it would be over and Mark would be gone. Out of her life. This time forever, she hoped. All she had to do was manage for a brief time.

"Hey." Dell's cheerful voice cut into her thoughts. "All set for a good time?"

She tried to smile at him. "All set to learn something new about the theater," she corrected.

Dell laughed. "Always the good little student, aren't you?"

Claudia shrugged. "Dr. Hanson did make it sound rather intriguing."

Dell's eyes sparkled with mischief. "The good Dr. Hanson could make anything sound intriguing, especially to a woman. I bet most of the females on this trip are more interested in the good professor than in his beloved drama. Speaking of which . . ." He lowered his voice to a whisper and leaned toward her. "The professor wouldn't make a bad actor himself. 'I love this theater,'" he repeated, lowering his tone to a fairly good approximation of Mark's. "'I want to share it with you.' Why, he almost brought tears to my eyes."

"It is possible to love one's work," Claudia replied sharply. Far too sharply, she realized when Dell gave her a strange look.

"Don't tell me the Ice Queen herself has fallen for our handsome professor?"

Claudia laughed. She'd known about the Ice Queen nickname for a long time now, and didn't mind it in the least. Her reputation for coldness had kept many men from approaching her—an effect which she had appreciated. "It would take more of a man than Dr. Hanson to throw me," she declared coldly. "He's not my type."

She turned to see how Dell was taking this, if he had believed her protective lie, and her eyes met those of Mark Hanson, who was working his way back toward the door. Something flickered there briefly in the depths of those dark eyes, but she could not identify it; and he moved on, his face a carefully controlled mask.

Fortunately, Dell was looking at her and did not notice who had passed by him. "Yes," Dell said. "I'm more your type."

The idea of ever seriously considering Dell as a romantic interest made her break into laughter. Though her laughter was at least half due to nervousness, Dell would never know it.

He smiled engagingly. "Yes," he continued. "I'm looking forward to this trip. It will give me a chance to get to know you better. You serious types need some fun. And I'm just the man for that."

"I'll keep that in mind," she replied dryly. "But right now, being one of those serious types, I want to study my guidebook."

3

~~~~~~~~~~~

Claudia stepped out of the shower in her Singapore hotel room and sighed. She was very grateful her father had seen to her having a room alone. After all those hours on the plane, hours in which Dell was always there, always chattering, she didn't need any more company. By rights, she should fall into that comfortable-looking bed and sleep off the effects of jet lag. But it was early afternoon in Singapore, and if she slept now she would be awake half the night. And she had slept some on the flight, too.

Dell's voice could almost be soothing once a person got used to it. Or perhaps she had just dozed in self-defense. At any rate, she didn't want to go to bed and there was nothing scheduled for the class until tomorrow.

She made a quick decision and reached for some

fresh clothes. There was a fascinating, different city right outside this hotel. And she was going out to look at it. Let the others sleep if they chose.

She ran a brush through her hair, outlined her mouth with a faint lipstick, and picked up her purse and guidebook. She would study the book in the elevator on the way to the lobby. There must be something of interest in the vicinity of the hotel. Then she smiled to herself. Everything would be of interest in this new place.

The elevator door opened as she was trying to orient herself on the map in the front of the guidebook. She looked up long enough to step off and head toward a vacant chair. Then her eyes went back to the map.

"Claudia!"

The guidebook slipped from her suddenly numb fingers as she looked up again and saw Mark Hanson.

"Let me get that." He bent quickly to retrieve it. "I'm sorry if I startled you," he said softly. "I was across the lobby and saw you getting off the elevator. Are you going out to see the city?"

She considered lying to him, but he was holding her guidebook in his hands. Her eyes went quickly to those strong hands. "I . . . I was only going to take a look around outside the hotel." She forced herself to meet his eyes. "I . . . I just wasn't sleepy."

Her heart was pounding in her throat and she clutched her purse tightly with both hands to still their trembling. What she should do was just take her guidebook and leave. She searched her mind for the right words, but none would come.

"Singapore is a fascinating city," Mark said. "Many

cultures meet and mix here. Chinese, Malay, Indian, Pakistani, Ceylonese. Many religions, too. Buddhist, Hindu, Moslem, Taoist. They call the city the melting pot of Asia."

Claudia nodded. Perhaps if they talked about the city she could get over this stupid nervousness, and the even stupider desire to reach out and touch the man so near her. "Some of the city looks very European," she said, then wondered if that sounded silly. "I mean, there seem to be a lot of skyscrapers."

Mark smiled. "Singapore is a city-state, a separate political entity. The whole island only covers something like twenty-five square miles, and with over two million people, they have to build up. There's nowhere else to go. A lot of the buildings you saw are high-rise apartment houses. They've been having a campaign for good housing. Trying to get rid of some of the bad living conditions."

He frowned. "In the past many people lived on the street. Or whole families shared a seven-by-seven room, without even an outside window. But listen, why are we standing here talking? Let me show you something of the city."

"I . . . can't." She stammered and felt foolish about it. Part of her—a big part, too—wanted very much to go with him, to pretend, as he seemed to be doing, that that long-ago weekend had never happened. Being with him made her feel young and carefree, eighteen again. But, reminded another part of her, she had sworn never to let herself get hurt like that again.

"Why not?" Mark asked. "I'm a very good guide. I know this city like the back of my hand."

"I . . ." Desperately she tried to think of something, anything, that she could use as an excuse, but her mind refused to cooperate. "I . . ." she began again. "All right." Her sudden capitulation came as a surprise even to her.

He grinned and slipped her guidebook into his pocket. "Remind me to return this to you later," he said. "You won't need it when you have me."

He offered her his arm. Again the two parts of her mind battled, but her body made the decision and she slipped her arm through his, biting her lip to keep from uttering a little sound of pleasure as she touched him.

He glanced down at her feet and smiled. "I see you're wearing low-heeled, comfortable shoes, so we can walk."

"Of course."

"I want you to have a ride in a trishaw, too. A kind of cross between a rickshaw and a bicycle," he explained. "Are you a bargain hunter?" he asked. "Do you want to take home some souvenirs?"

She shrugged. "I might buy something, but only if it's something I like. Maybe a piece of jade for my father. Nothing fancy or really expensive," she added, "but nice. And not machine made."

He squeezed her arm. "Then the Thieves' Market will be our first stop. You can buy anything there, from a pearl to a motorcycle."

By this time they had reached the sidewalk outside the hotel. Claudia gasped. After the hotel's air-conditioned comfort, the air assailed her lungs almost like an enemy, it was so hot and heavy.

"High humidity here," Mark said. "These are tropical latitudes. Just take it easy. You'll get used to it."

Claudia took a deep breath. "Does it ever get cold here?"

Mark shook his head. "Not really. It's always hot and humid."

"I see." She smiled. She couldn't help herself. She felt like a young girl, only much happier and more alive than she had felt as a girl—except, of course, for that one weekend. Being with Mark did things to her, made her aware of feelings she usually kept buried.

Perhaps this sightseeing trip was a mistake. Perhaps it was going to be too disturbing for her to be with Mark. But, she reminded herself, the whole tour was just an interlude. A brief interlude. What harm could there be in enjoying a day in the company of an attractive man? Wasn't that what her father had intended when he told her to relax and have fun?

She was older now, more capable of controlling her feelings. She was no longer going to fall eagerly into a man's arms, not even those of Mark Hanson. That lesson she had learned well and painfully. If he wanted to while away the day by showing her the sights of this strange and different city, she would let him. She certainly would not let him do anything else.

"Why do they call it the Thieves' Market?" she asked brightly, determined to keep this impersonal conversation alive.

"In the old days," he explained as they moved slowly down the street, "the city was not so law abiding as it is now. Robbery was a rather common occurrence. If thieves took something of yours, there was a good chance you could come across it in the Thieves' Market in the next several days. Then you could buy it back."

"That's appalling."

Mark shrugged. "Things are different now. But the

name stuck after the practice vanished. There are so many people in the city now that laws must be passed and obeyed. Have you noticed how clean everything is?" He gestured toward the street.

"No, but now that you mention it . . ."

"Ordinances against littering are strictly enforced," he explained. "Otherwise they'd soon be buried under the rubbish."

He paused suddenly to avoid running into someone ahead of them. Her fingers closed automatically on the hard muscles of his arm as she came to an abrupt stop against his side, her breast pressed against his arm. The contact shook her, made her whole body pulse with a longing so strong that for a moment she could only stand there, helpless under its onslaught.

She cast around in her mind for something to say, some topic of conversation to take her mind off these forbidden feelings. "Do . . . do Asian peoples have more respect for authority than, say, Americans?" she asked. "I mean, the other day when you were talking about Oedipus and tragedy, you said that they are fatalistic."

Mark nodded. "Yes. I guess that's true. Generally speaking, at least. Americans, you know, are a very individualistic people. It seems to be a part of our national heritage." He smiled down at her. "I suppose that it has worked to our advantage. After all, we had a big, rough country to tame, and it was the individualists who did it."

His expression became more serious. "But from experience in other, different cultures, I've discovered something else, something we lack. The people around here, in Malaysia and Indonesia, have better methods of working together. Oh, it's true that we Americans always come through in a crisis. Give us a tangible enemy, a real threat, and we'll pull together, we'll lick it—or them. Here they do that all the time. In Indonesia, for example, they practice a kind of village democracy. Every man has a seat on the village council. And they all must agree before anything is done."

Claudia stared at him. "You can't be serious."

"Oh, but I am. The name for this village system is *gotang royong*. Another thing, a man must be married to take his place as an adult. Only married men are considered suitable for responsibility."

Claudia shook her head. She didn't intend to ask about the fate of unmarried women. "It sounds very different."

"It is. But some of it makes a lot of sense. And some of it isn't so very different. Take *adat*, for instance."

"And what is *adat*?" she asked. She realized she was spending far more time looking at him than at the teeming city around her, but she couldn't help it. Her eyes were constantly drawn to him.

"It can be translated roughly as 'custom.' Only, in these parts it carries a lot more weight. One of our individualists wouldn't think too long before defying custom to pursue something very important to him. But an Asian would. *Adat* is stronger than law. It's one of the reasons these cultures are so slow to change. If it's always been done that way, it's *adat*. And there's no going against it. The good of the community always comes before the good of the individual."

Claudia considered this. "That could be rather dangerous. The individual doesn't seem to have any rights at all."

Mark shrugged. "Our way goes wrong sometimes, too. Maybe what's needed is a happy medium."

She frowned. "If that could ever be achieved."

"Well," he said, squeezing her arm again, "that's enough seriousness for today. We're going to relax and enjoy ourselves. And to that end—" He stopped and whistled shrilly. From the middle of the crowded street an empty trishaw came zooming toward the curb.

As Mark helped her into the seat, Claudia glanced at the slender young man who stood ready to pedal it—and them. He hardly looked strong enough to move himself, let alone two other people.

Mark settled down beside her. "Thieves' Market," he said.

The next thing she knew they were out in the street, weaving between cars and pedestrians at what seemed a breakneck speed. She tried to laugh as she was thrown against him and had to clutch his arm. "This is more thrilling than a roller coaster ride."

"And possibly more dangerous," said Mark as the driver slipped between two cars and in front of another. "But these drivers are really good. Stronger than they look, too." He gestured toward the buildings they were passing. "I'd like to have booked us into there, the Raffles Hotel. It's a landmark. Very impressive facade. Named for Sir Stamford Raffles."

"Who founded Singapore," she finished.

"Well, the English think so," Mark replied. "Actually there were cities here before Sir Stamford came upon the place. But Sir Stamford did see its mercantile potential. The English are always good at that."

Claudia nodded. "I've been noticing bright banners outside some of the buildings. Are those Chinese letters?" What she was trying not to notice was the way his thigh pressed against hers, making her whole body tremble.

"Yes. Some are shop signs. They give the city color, don't they?"

"I like them much better than neon."

"Yes, so do I. But there are neon signs in some parts of town. Young people wear cowboy boots and ride motorcycles. The Malays seem to be the most affected by the encroachment of civilization. The Chinese family structure is still very strong, though it is weakening gradually."

The trishaw driver was weaving in and out with a rapidity that turned the city around them into so many separate flashing scenes. Claudia was hard put not to succumb to a wave of dizziness brought on by his quick changes of direction. Suddenly he darted off the road and came to an abrupt halt by the sidewalk.

"Well," Mark said. "Here we are. Thieves' Market." He pulled out his wallet and paid the trishaw man. Then he took her hand. She considered pulling it away, but somehow she could not.

"Now, what would you like to look at?" he asked.

"Everything," she replied with a breathless little laugh.

"OK. We'll just meander around."

"I'd like that." Her hand was still in his, but she knew now that she wasn't going to try to remove it. She did not allow herself to think about why.

Together they started down one of the aisles. To each side of them stood and sat various merchants, their wares laid out, some on little tables, some on the ground itself. She laughed. Side by side stood a large display of shining hubcaps and a table of jade figurines.

Mark smiled. "The mixing of East and West seems rather amusing at times." He moved closer to examine a jade elephant, then stepped back to her side. "Not what you want," he said.

Claudia smiled. "It's good to have an expert's advice."

He pulled her closer to his side and her heart began to pound again. She hurried on, trying to ignore the warmth of this body against hers. "I'd like to get Dad one of those laughing Buddha figures. The ones with the potbellies you rub for luck."

Mark looked grave. "I'm not sure that's a very representative gift."

"No, of course not." She felt flustered. She hadn't really wanted the little laughing figure. It was only something to say, something to distract her mind from the feelings of her body. "What do you suggest?"

"Maybe a jade elephant. Elephants are used in Malaya still. They do a lot of heavy work in the jungle."

"Yes, that's right. Let's get him a jade elephant. Not too big," she continued, wondering if she should try to pull her hand loose. It was hard to think straight while he was touching her, but she let her hand remain.

He moved her on down the aisle, and the marvels of the bazaar continued to unfold around them. A young Malay in leather jacket and cowboy boots argued the merits of a shining Harley-Davidson with a sober Chinese merchant in a business suit. In the next space, an old Hindu in turban and loincloth squatted amid a collection of battered cooking pans. Beyond him, a long trestle table shimmered with bolts of silk. Claudia stopped to touch the lovely material. "So many colors," she breathed softly. A middle-aged Chinese woman in a tight-fitting, high-necked, sleeveless orange gown materialized suddenly. "Would the American lady like to have a *sari*? Like Indian ladies wear? Or a *cheongsam*, perhaps?" She indicated her own gown.

"Oh, no, thank you," Claudia stammered quickly. The cheongsam, for all its high neck and long skirt, was one of the most provocative gowns she had ever seen. She would never dream of exposing her body in such a way.

Mark blocked her effort to move on. "I think you'd look very nice in a cheongsam," he said. "But I'll settle for a sari. Which material do you like?"

She shook her head. "I don't know how to wrap one."

"American lady will have no trouble," the clerk said firmly. "I give paper that tells how to wrap. You pick silk."

He looked at her expectantly, but she just shook her head. "I can't."

"Then I will. Now, let me see." He turned to the clerk. "What do you recommend?"

Claudia colored under the scrutiny of a pair of dark almond eyes. "Pale blue or green," the clerk said. "I have one. Blue and green together. Very pretty on this lady." She moved swiftly down the line of bolts. "This one."

Claudia caught her breath. The silk was semitransparent; the color of sea-foam, it was shot through with silver threads.

Mark held the loose end of the bolt up to her face.

He nodded. "Yes, that's just the thing. Cut us a length for a sari."

She knew she should protest. Paper of instructions aside, she was never going to wear a sari. But the words would not come. The material was really beautiful. She could surely find some use for it. And, to put it quite simply, she just plain wanted it.

She dug down into her purse for her money, but Mark stopped her. "This is on me," he said.

She shook her head. "I can't allow that," she said firmly. "This will be my souvenir. Now if you'll just help me find some jade for Dad, I'll be very grateful."

"All right."

To her intense relief, he did not pursue the subject any further, and they moved on down the aisle, the package under his arm.

On both sides of them were displayed some of the strangest assortments of merchandise that Claudia had ever seen. New items and old were mixed indiscriminately, from potato peelers to car jacks to giant temple jars and brass-inlaid tables. A buyer could find anything and everything here.

She sniffed. The smell of something delicious was coming through the air. Her mouth watered as she turned to Mark. "What smells so good?"

"*Satay.* Come on, we'll have some." And he made his way across the crowded aisle to where a Malay was cooking skewers of meat over a tiny brazier.

Mark got two sticks from the vendor and handed her one. "What's in it?" she asked, sinking her teeth into a crisp piece of meat.

"Chicken, lamb and beef," Mark replied, offering her some sauce on a leaf. "This is peanut sauce. Spicy, but good."

"Ummmm." The crispy, tender meat had a unique flavor. She hadn't realized how hungry she was.

She finished hers and looked around for a place to throw the empty stick. Mark extended his hand. "Give it to me. Can you eat another?"

"Oh, yes. It was delicious." The second stick of meat disappeared almost as quickly as the first. Claudia returned the empty stick to Mark. "The litter laws must be very strict," she commented.

Mark grinned. "They are," he conceded. "But that's not the idea here. I need the sticks to pay for our snack. They're the check, so to speak." And while she watched, he presented the sticks to the vendor and was told how much to pay.

Mark took her hand again as they moved on. And she let him. There were a great many people crowding the Thieves' Market, she told herself. And, though she supposed she could find her way back to the hotel if they got separated, she would certainly prefer not to have to do so. A poor excuse is better than none at all, said a sharp warning voice from her mind, but she ignored it.

More and more displays of goods unfolded before them. They stopped once to examine a huge selection of brass vases and candlesticks. At another place an artist had set up shop and was doing portraits in chalk.

As they stood watching the likeness take form, she remembered times at the amusement park in the summer, when she'd seen couples getting pictures of themselves together.

The idea had seemed very romantic at the time, as though the picture were a kind of permanent reminder of young love. But that had been before her weekend with Mark. Later she had changed her mind. Such a thing would only be another painful relic, and she had had more than enough of those.

Mark pulled at her hand. "Hey, come back."

She managed a smile. That had been long ago, when she'd been young and foolish. She knew better now. She knew enough to enjoy a day for what it was. Just one day. No future to it.

Mark stopped before a display of jewelry. Ornate and intricate, it looked old. There was one piece especially that took her eye. The green stone in the ring was square cut. It was far too big to be a real emerald and she did not wear much jewelry, but she did like the look of it.

"See something you like?" Mark asked, shifting the package of material he had tucked under his arm.

"It's all very beautiful," she said quickly. "But there's nothing special."

For a moment he looked as though he didn't believe her, but he said no more and they moved on.

"Wait here," he said as they neared a table that held a conglomeration of items. It seemed as though this dealer had a little of everything. Claudia watched as Mark plucked a little jade elephant from between a rusty can opener and a spray of faded plastic roses. Somewhat to her surprise, he didn't turn to her, but approached the merchant, a Chinese of indeterminate age.

What happened then was intriguing. She had read enough in her guidebook to realize that Mark was bargaining. Otherwise, she might easily have supposed that their spirited discussion, which was punctuated with rather violent gestures and words that sounded suspiciously like curses, was in danger of leading to a real fight. As it was, however, all the noise was just that—noise. And eventually Mark rejoined her carrying the little jade elephant in a much creased paper bag.

He smiled triumphantly. "I made a good deal."

"You certainly look like you enjoyed yourself."

He grinned. "I did. Bargaining is an Eastern art. Everyone does it here."

Several more times that afternoon she had the opportunity to watch him in action, and each time he returned to her side triumphantly to show her his find.

The afternoon flew by. Claudia couldn't believe how late it was when she finally thought to look at her watch.

Mark saw the gesture and repeated it. "It is late, isn't it? Time always flies when you're having fun. Listen, I have a great idea. The afternoon may be gone, but the night's young yet. Let's have dinner together. I know a great little Chinese place. Superb Cantonese food."

"I . . . I'm a student, remember?" she stammered, then flushed as she realized she should have thought of this much earlier. "Students aren't supposed to . . . to fraternize with professors."

"I haven't once thought of you as a student," he said. "Not the entire afternoon. Besides, I'm only asking you to dinner. After all, professors and students do eat. And sometimes together. You're auditing, too, so you won't even be getting a grade."

"I . . . I know that, but the rest of the class doesn't. I don't want to undermine class morale." She tried to smile. "The role of teacher's pet isn't a very comfortable one."

He shook his head. "You're not very good at this kind of thing, Claudia. You may be a drama major, but acting isn't your thing. If you don't want to have dinner with me, just say so. Don't give me transparent excuses."

"I . . ." She was not capable of voicing the lie. She did want to have dinner with him. The day had been practically perfect. She couldn't remember when she'd last had so much fun. She was an adult now, capable of taking stock of things. She was no longer a starry-eyed teenager living in a romantic fairy tale. She knew now that a good time was only that—a good time. Not the start of something else.

"I would like to have dinner with you," she said finally. "Thank you for asking me."

4

The Chinese restaurant was small. Beribboned lanterns cast a soft glow over the little white-covered tables and secluded booths. Mark smiled at her across the flickering candle. "Have you a preference or do you want me to order for both of us?"

The memory came back to her, swift and sharp. He had asked the same question in the same way many long years ago. She could see in his face the same eagerness, the same desire to please. For a moment she felt as she had then, before the betrayal, before the pain, when life had been new and beautiful. Because of him.

She swallowed over the lump in her throat and said the same thing she had said then. "You choose for me."

Did he remember? she wondered. Had he deliberately tried to evoke old memories? Or was this his normal manner of dealing with a woman? It didn't really matter, she reminded herself. Her goal was to enjoy one day at a time. Her future was already laid out—crystal clear. This trip, this day, this brief interlude with Mark had nothing to do with that. This was only for now.

"OK." Mark addressed the tiny waitress who was clad in a turquoise cheongsam. "We'll start with sweet and sour soup. Egg rolls. Then chicken almond ding for the lady and moo goo gai pan for me."

"Yes, sir."

As the waitress retreated, moving in short gliding steps, Claudia glanced around the room. Somehow, on the street, in the sunshine and among the crowds of people, things had been easier. This was too much like the dinner that had led to her mistake. The dim lights and intimate atmosphere did nothing to help her fight Mark's appeal. If anything, he was more attractive now than he had been at twenty-six, while she . . . She could tell herself all the nice things she could think of about maturity and such, but the fact remained. She was thirty years old and still unmarried. He must find that rather odd. And although she took care of herself physically, she was no longer a fresh and dewy eighteen.

"So," he said, leaning across the tiny table while his dark eyes searched hers, "what do you think of Thieves' Market?"

"It's fabulous," she replied, grateful for this neutral topic. "I've been to flea markets at home, but I've never seen anything to equal this. And Dad will be pleased with his jade elephant." She patted her bag. "Thank you for helping me find it."

"You're quite welcome," he said softly. His eyes were warm as they gazed into hers.

Deliberately she pulled hers away, made them survey the room. It contained a cosmopolitan crowd. Women in saris and cheongsams mingled with those in Western dress of all styles, from simple blue jeans to the chicest evening gowns. Most of the men wore Western dress—jeans, slacks, or business suits.

The little waitress brought the soup, and Claudia busied herself with eating. It was rather more spicy than her palate was accustomed to, but she found it delicious.

"I wish we had more time here," Mark said. "There are so many things I'd like to show you. Chinese and Buddhist and Moslem temples. The Botanical Gardens. The Tiger Balm Gardens built by the Aw brothers, a sort of oriental Disneyland with life-sized figures from Chinese mythology."

"It's certainly a fascinating city," she agreed, hoping that her voice did not betray the avalanche of emotion that had washed over her with the words "I want to show you." He loved the city, that was all, and he liked to show it to people. The words had no more meaning than that.

As she chewed her chicken almond ding, she tried to concentrate on the food and the restaurant's atmosphere, but the table was very small and Mark was very close. There ought to be some way she could stop the feelings he aroused in her. Feelings she didn't want. But so far she was unable to find any.

A noise to her right drew her attention, and she turned that way just as what she had believed to be a solid wall was folded back to reveal another large area. More tables were clustered around a little space for dancing, and in one corner sat a group of musicians. The soft strains of dance music began to drift across the room. It was thoroughly Western music—songs by Cole Porter, Lerner and Loewe, and other Americans —but the musicians were clearly Chinese.

"An added attraction," Mark said.

She smiled. "American music in a Chinese restuarant?"

He shrugged. "Singapore is a tourist-conscious town. Many tourists are American. Besides, our music is appreciated the world over. When this group, which plays what we at home call 'slow dance' music, takes its intermissions, there'll be musical acts from other cultures." He smiled. "Have you heard much oriental music?"

She shook her head. "I'm afraid not, Mark." She spoke his name unawares. She had not intended to use it. Not with all those memories of whispering it against his ear during their kisses and embraces so long ago. But he didn't seem to notice. "I'm afraid all my knowledge of music, which I'd be the first to admit is relatively scanty, has to do with the European variety."

"That's not unusual. Tomorrow at the Chinese street opera, or later when we see the puppet show, you'll hear a different kind of music. To Western ears it seems rather strident, even unmusical, but if you give it a chance, you may come to like it."

She hoped he would keep talking about things like this. It seemed safer that way. "You certainly know a lot about these cultures."

He smiled. "As I told the class, these arts are all connected. You can't know the theater without knowing the history, the music, the dance, the customs of the people involved. Theater here, and in the places we're going to visit, is made up of all these elements. You just can't separate them."

"What prompted you to take up such a complex subject?" she asked, trying not to let her longing for him show in her eyes. "Did you do your dissertation on it?"

For a moment a strange look, a look almost of pain, crossed his face. Then he reached for his coffee cup, and when he looked at her again that look was gone.

"In high school I always liked drama. The excitement of a live performance. The intriguing relationship between audience and performers. I was a drama major in college when I enlisted for Vietnam." His expression grew serious. "There wasn't much drama being performed there, wartime being what it is. But I became intrigued with the people, the culture. And as I made friends, I learned about their theater. After the war, I talked my profs into letting me do my work on Southeast Asian drama and came over here to do research."

His expression lightened. "It's such a wide-open field that I didn't have much competition." His smile became boyish. "So I managed to get tenure and a full professorship in spite of the delay in my education."

"I see." He had made no mention of his wife or her family and she realized that she was relieved. Apparently he didn't want to discuss them. Certainly she didn't want to hear about them.

She finished her meal and sat back with a sigh. "That was delicious."

"I'm glad you enjoyed it. How about a dance or two while we wait for our fortune cookies?"

"I . . ." The blood rushed to her cheeks and she was grateful for the dimness of the candlelight.

"Please," he urged. "I haven't spent such a pleasant day in a long, long time. Just a couple of dances before we go back to the hotel."

She found herself getting to her feet. Her mind might insist that dancing with this man was madness, but her body yearned for the feel of his arms around her. He didn't say any more, but took her hand and led her toward the little dance floor.

His arm slid around her naturally, as naturally as it had those long years ago. All her senses seemed heightened. Her left hand could feel the hardness of his shoulder under the smooth fabric of his lightweight jacket. Her right hand, clasped in his, could feel the strength and power in his long fingers. His chin rested against her cheek, the beginning of his beard lightly prickling against her skin. His arm tightened around her, and her breasts, which had been just touching the front of his jacket, came in closer contact with him. His hard thighs brushed against her as they danced.

A sigh worked its way up from deep inside her and she swallowed over the lump in her throat. They had danced like this before, too. Everything seemed to be conspiring to remind her of the past. A sensible person, of course, would remember the pain and shun the man who had caused it. And she did remember the pain. But even more vividly, she remembered the joy, the intensity of living that she had felt with him, as though all the world were suddenly brighter and finer because of his existence in it.

His lips were near her ear. She felt the soft touch of his breath as he whispered, "Beautiful music, isn't it?"

"Yes." She was glad he could not see her face, could not spot the tears she was blinking back. There was only now, she kept reminding herself. The past was over—dead. And the future was yet to be. What she must think of now was the present, only the present. Enjoy it for what it was. One pleasant afternoon. One pleasant evening. The past and the future were both irrelevant.

As they moved slowly in time to the music, she clung to these thoughts. But try as she might to discipline her mind, her body refused to behave. The feel of his body so close to hers did more than conjure up memories. It roused feelings in her that were very much in the here and now. Feelings that would have to be dealt with before this night was over.

The orchestra finished its number and began another, but Mark made no move to leave the dance floor and she did not suggest it. If she could have had her wish, it would have been for a way to prolong this innocent pleasure. Being in his arms was satisfying in itself. She had not danced for many years. Although she still enjoyed dancing, too many men seemed to view it as a mere preliminary to other, more serious business.

They danced through two more numbers before Mark led her back to the table. Two dishes of orange ice and a pair of fortune cookies were delivered by the little waitress seconds after they reached their seats. Mark extended the plate with the cookies. "You first."

She chose the one nearest her, holding it, reluctant to break it and discover its message.

Mark snapped his open and withdrew the little curl of paper. He read silently, then smiled. "Good luck attends your efforts," he repeated.

She managed a smile, too. "Well, that certainly applies to your career."

He nodded. "Now read yours."

She laughed nervously. "I don't believe in this kind of thing."

"Of course not," he agreed. "It's just for fun. But read it."

Her fingers trembled as she broke open the cookie and withdrew the little slip.

"Shall I read it for you?" he asked as she still hesitated.

She nodded, letting him take it from her fingers.

"Old friends are the best kind," he read, his face serious, his eyes warm on hers.

She wanted to make some kind of reply, to joke away this moment of tension between them, but her mind seemed paralyzed. Nothing would work properly.

He let the piece of paper fall to his plate. "Ready?" he asked.

"Yes. Thank you." She really did not want to go, to leave this place of safety where she had allowed herself to relax a little, but they couldn't stay there all night. Sooner or later they would have to leave.

As they stepped out of the restaurant, he tucked her arm through his. The street was bright; she blinked against the glare of flashing neon. As a tourist town, Singapore offered a great deal of night life.

"Shall we take a cab or walk?" he asked.

"Is it far?"

"Five or six blocks."

"Let's walk then. I enjoy seeing the town."

"Fine."

The street was crowded. Claudia looked around,

admiring a slender Indian woman in a flowing yellow sari. "I wonder how they keep them on."

Mark chuckled and patted the package under his arm. "Your paper will tell you."

She laughed, and heard the nervousness in it. "I just can't imagine wearing one."

"I think you can wear anything you choose," he said softly. "And wear it very well."

Embarrassment washed over her again, and so did memories of the admiration in his eyes when he had first looked at her naked body. A look very much like what was on his face now.

"Thank you," she managed to mumble, then turned away, pretending to study the area around her.

A thin, reedy sound came piercing through the murmur of the crowd. Claudia grabbed at the diversion. "What kind of music is that?"

Mark smiled. "Sounds like a snake charmer."

She turned to him with startled eyes. "Really?"

"Really," he affirmed. "You can still see them around. It's a way to make a living."

She shivered. "What kind of snakes?"

"Hooded cobras are just about sinister enough," he said. "Let's go take a look."

Before she could think of any excuses, he was propelling her down the street and through the crowd. There, in the circle of light spread by a streetlamp, a dark, wizened little man sat cross-legged. A soiled turban covered his head, and a loincloth was wrapped around his waist, but his chest was bare and so thin that she could count every rib.

A considerable crowd had gathered, but everyone stayed a respectable distance from the covered basket that reposed in front of the man. He reached out a scrawny arm and tipped off the lid. Then he raised a flutelike instrument to his mouth.

The same thin, reedy sound came plaintively through the air, but now all eyes were on that uncovered basket. The crowd took a collective breath as the cobra's head appeared over the rim and two glittering eyes gleamed in the evil-looking face.

Unable to help herself, Claudia pressed closer to Mark's side. His arm went around her protectively and she felt the warmth of arousal creeping through her again.

The snake charmer swayed in rhythm to the strange music, and the cobra, which seemed balanced on its tail, swayed too. Claudia shivered again. What a horrible way to make a living!

Mark glanced down at her. "Seen enough?"

She tried to laugh. "Too much, I'm afraid. I hope I don't see that monster in my dreams."

He seemed about to say something, then checked himself and merely nodded, pulling her out of the crowd and on down the street.

It really wasn't far to the hotel, and she found herself wishing it were much further. Being with him was exhilarating. He was like some exotic drink that went to her head and made her feel all bubbly inside. But, she reminded herself, like such a drink, his effect would wear off. And too many such "drinks" would leave her with a hung-over heart. She thought the metaphor rather apt and wished she had someone to share it with.

The hotel loomed up before them and she caught back a sigh. She didn't want this evening to end. She didn't want to leave him. But an interlude was just that. And she had to remember it.

They were silent as they entered the hotel. She realized that he had dropped her hand as they drew nearer. Walking through the lobby, they might have been mere acquaintances, and in the elevator, with strangers sharing the ride, they said little.

As the elevator door closed behind them, she grew increasingly nervous. Some of the other students also had rooms on that floor. Outside her door, she turned to him. "Thank you, Mark." She had not meant to say his name again. The sound of it tore at her heart and made her hesitate. "I . . . appreciate your showing me the city."

His smile was subdued and his dark eyes warm as he put her package into her hands. "It was my pleasure, Claudia. I only wish we had more time. I wish . . ."

Her heart jumped up into her throat. If he asked to come in, to renew their old intimacy . . . She should tell him no. Let him suffer a little. But she didn't know if she had the strength to resist him. Her mind was quite clear on the subject: it was sheer stupidity even to consider sleeping with him again. But her body disagreed with that.

She knew she was intoxicated with his physical nearness. The chemical attraction between them was as strong as ever. Her body, which had lain dormant over the long years, was rebelling now. It had been content to be kept under control, to be unresponsive to the advances of men. But this was different. This was the man whose touch had wakened her sleeping sexuality—her Prince Charming. And her body refused to heed the warning that her mind was so desperately screaming.

His eyes met hers, and she knew her eyes were

wide with expectancy. She felt the quivering of her lower lip and was powerless to control it. She could think of nothing to say, nothing that would not be either dangerous or inane.

"Claudia," he began, his voice deep and throaty. "I . . ."

She waited, hardly daring to breath, hoping and yet fearing that he would ask.

His face reflected indecision. Then suddenly he pulled her to him and her package fell unheeded to the floor. She did not intend to resist his kiss, indeed, had no strength to do so. But even if she had, he gave her no chance. She was crushed against his chest, kept there by the strength of one arm, while the other hand tilted her chin upward and his mouth covered hers.

It was a brief kiss, but the first touch of his lips softened hers in response. She could no more stop herself from wrapping her arms around his neck and returning it than she could keep from remembering what their earlier kisses had led to.

When he released her and stepped back, it was all she could do to keep her feet. She stared at him.

"Good night, Claudia." For a long moment his eyes searched hers. "I like the woman you've become." He took a tentative step toward her, then seemed to change his mind and bent to retrieve her package and shove it at her. He wheeled on his heel. "See you tomorrow," he called back over his shoulder as he hurried away.

She did not move until he had disappeared around the corner of the corridor. It took a long time before she could manage her trembling fingers well enough to dig out the key from the depths of her purse and get it into the lock.

Once inside the room, she put the package on the bed and sank down into a chair. There was no use denying it. She really wished he had asked to come in with her. Her aroused body was clamoring for his touch. She wanted the sight of his face, the pressure of his hand, the sound of his voice. God help her, she wanted his love.

She jumped from the chair and began to pace the little room. She was being foolish. She was a grown woman now, not a romantic, love-struck teenager. Undoubtedly there was a physical attraction between them. But that was all it was—a sexual thing. Love was something else, something more. And it had no place in her life. She had her career. True, it offered no heady, drunken exhilaration, just the promise of a sane, stable, productive life. And that was what she wanted: stability, sensible contentments.

Love, with all its heady enchantment, could end only in pain. Surely experience had taught her that.

Absently, her thoughts still in turmoil, she undressed and stepped into the shower. As the water cascaded over her still-firm body, she caught herself wondering what he would think of it now. It was no longer unawakened. He had seen to that. With a muttered exclamation, she reached for the soap. If she didn't stop this kind of thinking, she would never get to sleep.

Maybe she should just stay away from him for the rest of this trip. Maybe even a brief interlude was too long to spend with him, was too dangerous. But she did need some rest and relaxation. It would do her good to forget the dissertation for a little while. From this distance she could see that her father had been right. She'd been going stale, working too hard. It was fun to be with Mark. Maybe she should just admit that and enjoy it. People could have fun together without anything serious coming out of it. That was Mark's philosophy. Why shouldn't it be hers? Enjoy today and let tomorrow take care of itself.

When she slid between the sheets, she was no nearer to making a decision. One moment she meant never to go near the man again, and the next she wanted to feel his arms around her. And when finally she fell asleep, it was to dream of dancing close to Mark—a lovely dance that went on and on for as long as she pleased.

5

~∞∞∞∞∞∞∞∞∞∞~

The next morning when Claudia got off the elevator in the lobby to meet the group, she looked immediately for Dell. The cold light of day had convinced her that being with Mark was too dangerous. It was like playing with fire, and she had already been burned once.

"Hi there, beautiful." Dell took her hand. "Where'd you disappear to yesterday? I kept calling and calling you."

"I wanted to see the city," she said, easing her hand out of his grip. "It's a fascinating place."

"Yeah."

She was about to ask him about his evening, but something about his expression of satisfaction put her off. She was pretty sure there were sections of Singapore and activities of Dell's that she would prefer to know nothing about.

She glanced toward the elevator. She was not at all anxious to see Mark. Last night she had been in a kind of daze, an intoxication brought on by the man's physical nearness and the burning memories of their earlier times together. But this was daylight, a time for common sense to prevail. And common sense dictated that she stay as far as possible from Mark Hanson. There was no point in repeating the painful past.

She pushed nervously at her hair and adjusted the beige shoulder bag that she habitually carried because it went with just about anything. If only there were some way she could avoid seeing Mark. If she became suddenly ill . . . But then he might come up to the room to see how she was. A wave of warmth rushed over her body at the thought of Mark in her room . . . and what could so easily happen there.

"So today we see a puppet show," Dell said. "And this is supposed to be a graduate seminar." He laughed and shook his head. "I hope the old man doesn't find that out. I'm afraid he'd think puppets kind of childish."

It was on the tip of her tongue to tell him that in that case their study was quite appropriate for him, but just then the elevator door opened and she caught a glimpse of Mark stepping out. She averted her face quickly, turning so that her back was toward the elevator. "Culture comes in many forms," she told Dell, trying to smile. "You should know that by now."

"Oh, I do, I do. I'm the original culture vulture."

Her smile widened. "Oh, Dell, will you ever grow up?"

He laughed. "Not if I can help it." And, emboldened by her smile, he put a friendly arm around her waist.

At that precise moment Mark came into view. She couldn't help herself; her eyes sought his, hoping for some look, some sign, some recognition of the night before. But nothing appeared to be different. His face remained that of the scholar and teacher. "If you'll join the rest of the group"—he indicated where the other students had gathered—"I'll give you some background on what we're going to see today."

"Yes, sir."

Dell's cheerful reply made Claudia want to grit her teeth. Why did seeing Dell in Mark's company make Dell seem foolishly juvenile? As they crossed the lobby, she managed to ease away from Dell's arm.

"Now," Mark said to the group gathered around him. "We're going to observe a Chinese street opera. Don't let the word 'opera' fool you. It won't sound at all like the opera you know."

He glanced around the group. "Chinese music, like much of the music in this part of the world, is based on dissonance. That means that to our ears, which are accustomed to consonance and harmony, it will sound tinny, shrill, out of key. Nothing like music as you know it. Nevertheless, it is music. And a vital part of this drama.

"The street opera is very old," he continued. "The stories are well known. And even if they weren't, the audience could always recognize the villains."

"How?" asked one of the students.

"You remember the old cowboy movies. How did you tell the good guys from the bad ones?"

"The good guys wore the white hats."

Mark nodded. "Right. The same idea applies here. You can tell a player's character by the way his face is painted. For instance, black indicates loyalty, sincerity, bravery.

"As you watch, keep in mind that this is a highly stylized form. Everything—the music, the face paint, the way the actor walks, the movement of a single finger—is done in a particular way."

His eyes met Claudia's, then moved on. "In this theater there is no conflict between nature and art such as we find in the Shakespearian theater of the early nineteenth century. For the Chinese, theater is art. Gestures, paint, costumes, music—all done one way—the right way."

"How does such a theater grow?" asked a voice from the back of the group. "It sounds stagnant to me."

"A good question," Mark replied. "Other forms evolve. For instance, certain themes in current movies are reminiscent of the old stories. The warrior maiden of the street opera has a movie descendant. You can see her on the billboards. Her white painted face shows her goodness."

"I read somewhere that women were not allowed on the Chinese stage," said another student.

Mark nodded. Claudia admired the way he ran this class, the way he involved the students in the discussions. A lot of teachers didn't do that. "At one time they weren't. In China, as in England and America, acting was often considered a shady profession and women were kept from entering it. Consequently, some of China's greatest actors made their reputations by playing women."

Dell giggled and Claudia glanced at him in annoyance. Why couldn't he behave with some sense of dignity?

Mark simply ignored him. "Now, I have arranged for us to watch a performance near here. In deference to other members of the audience, I'll ask you to keep your questions until after the performance. Note anything unusual and try to look for distinguishing characteristics. What I would like in your papers is an overview of the drama you're going to see. I'd like to have you look for similarities and differences. You'll find both." He smiled. "And, if you'll keep an open mind, some fascinating forms of theater. Now, I suppose we'd better be going."

As the group moved out toward the street, Claudia was torn between conflicting emotions. A part of her was screaming to touch Mark, to renew the feelings of last night, while another was issuing terrible warnings of disaster. And to add to this, there was Dell with his constant chatter and his annoying chauvinistic comments about everything they passed. Several times she considered moving away from him, but everyone seemed to have paired off, and as she was more or less a loner, it would have been difficult to attach herself to another group.

So she tried to close her ears to Dell's rather senseless comments and look around her with observant eyes. Just the crowd of people on the street, the way they were dressed, was fascinating to her. Coming toward them was an Indian woman, her sleek black hair gleaming, her pale pink sari shot through with gold thread, a jewel glowing in her nostril. A few paces behind her was a lovely Eurasian girl in a pale green suit, her smooth ivory complexion and slightly slanted eyes giving her an exotic beauty. A middle-aged Indian in a business suit and carrying a briefcase wore a white turban around his head. An older

Chinese couple, dressed alike in blue pajama-like suits, hurried past.

There were tourists, of course, too. Claudia could recognize some of them easily. Their bold printed shirts and Bermuda shorts made them stand out in a way that made her uncomfortable. She had never considered herself chic, had never had the time or inclination to pay much attention to fashion, but she did try to be presentable. For instance, the pale blue pants suit she wore now was unassuming and practical, and surely as comfortable as those gaudy outfits so many tourists seemed to favor.

Of course, she reminded herself, not all American tourists were like that. Undoubtedly, there were many like herself who did not stand out in a crowd. It was the loud, gaudy ones who gave everyone a bad name.

The sudden roar of a motorcycle startled her and she jumped as it whizzed by, hugging the curb. She had a glimpse of two bodies, cowboy boots, leather jackets, and long black hair. A Malay youth and his girl, she thought, as the cycle dipped and darted through the traffic and disappeared.

"Just like home," commented Dell. "I wonder if there are any countries in the world that are still without the motorcycle."

"I devoutly hope so," she replied. "There must be some places left. Some tropical island, maybe."

Dell only laughed at this, and she wished Mark were there beside her. Mark would have something to say, something interesting, she was sure. No matter what the topic.

The street was getting more crowded and Dell took her hand. She didn't try to pull away. His touch meant nothing to her. Through the murmur of the crowd came the sound of clashing cymbals. "I suppose *that's* music," Dell observed sourly.

Claudia forced a smile. "Probably."

The group stopped where a crowd had gathered. A small circle of sidewalk was ringed by spectators, and in it two actors, their faces ferocious with black, blue, and red paint, were battling it out with swords. The brilliantly painted faces and vivid costumes assaulted the senses. This was a very visual drama, Claudia thought. Then one actor leaped right over the head of the other and she realized that these men must also be trained acrobats. Whirling and slashing, the characters fought, each meeting of swords heralded by the clash of the cymbals while a chorus kept up a kind of high-pitched chant.

Fascinated, Claudia watched the graceful, stylized gestures. So engrossed was she in the almost balletlike movements that when a voice came booming over the crowd, she jumped, startled. She was even more surprised when she realized she was hearing English. "The general knows that there is someone in his room," the voice said. "But it is night. The room is dark. He can see nothing."

Beside her Dell snickered, but Claudia was lost in the artistry of the thing. To present such a scene in the brilliant sunlight, or even on a well-lighted stage, and to make it believable was quite a feat. She saw that she needed to rethink her whole concept of theater. There was more required of the audience here than Coleridge's "willing suspension of disbelief." This kind of theater required the most active imaginative response from the audience. It was their imaginations that furnished the darkness, that made the scene workable.

When the performance was over, Claudia turned eagerly to Dell. "How fascinating."

He shrugged. "Looked more like the circus than serious drama. All that jumping around and jabbing at each other. And that unholy racket they call music."

She frowned. "It's just different. Listen, Dell. I want to ask you something. You've read the background material, haven't you?"

He nodded. "Yeah. What about it?"

"Well, do you think the theater grew from the puppet plays or do you think it was the other way around?"

Dell shrugged. "I don't know. I find it hard to take this puppet business seriously. Puppets are for kids."

Claudia swallowed her irritation. "These are not Punch and Judy characters," she reminded him. "These are kings, generals, gods. Important personages in the religious and social history of these places."

Dell's expression did not change. "Why don't you go discuss the question with Hanson?"

For one terrifying moment she thought Dell had seen them together. Her tongue felt double in size, and she turned away as though to look in a shop window. Then she realized that Dell wouldn't have been able to approach such a subject obliquely. He meant just what he said, no more.

"Don't be silly," she replied. Throwing a quick glance to where Mark stood, she saw a woman student on either side of him and realized the source of Dell's comment. "I'm on this trip for knowledge, not a grade."

"We should all be so lucky," observed Dell with a lifted eyebrow. "But if you insist on pursuing the subject, I'll give you my expert opinion. I think the theater came first. It's ridiculous to think of theater, even this kind, being the descendant of puppet plays."

Claudia shook her head. "I think you're wrong. The way the actors move in that stylized way reminds me of puppets. I think the puppet plays came first, and the theater after."

Dell frowned. "I haven't seen anything yet that *we* would call theater. But then, this whole place is so backward, I suppose they could have done that backwards, too."

Claudia stared at him in indignation. "I give up on you, Dell. Patriotism is one thing, but blind, pigheaded obstinance is another. You're not willing to give anything else a chance. Can't you see that art forms don't have to be right or wrong, better or worse? They can all be equally good—just different."

Dell grimaced in disgust. "Now you're beginning to sound like our beloved prof." He eyed her shrewdly. "You really don't mean to tell me that you think the wailing and cavorting we saw this morning surpasses one of Kean's performances of *Hamlet?*"

"Of course not." She saw the trap he had laid and neatly sidestepped it. "What I am saying is that such a performance is just as meaningful and important to the people of its culture as a performance of Hamlet was to Kean's England. You might also consider the fact that this theater is enjoyed by a larger proportion of the population than *Hamlet* is by modern Westerners."

Dell shook his head. "I don't understand you, Claudia. If I didn't know you so well, I'd think you were getting ready to butter up Hanson. But I know that's not your style. And besides, you aren't even getting a grade."

"I don't study just to get grades," she replied, trying to hide her sudden agitation. Dell was not the smartest man in the world, but she was afraid he had hit rather close to home. It was more than likely that her feelings for Mark had a lot to do with her willingness to be open-minded about these new forms of drama. Yet it was also true that she had always been interested in other cultures. Those others had been European, of course, but she had been completely unaware of the existence of forms such as they had seen that morning.

As the group re-formed around Mark, she wished suddenly that she had the courage to ask her question. And not for any other reason than that she was interested in the answer. It was certainly clear enough that she didn't need to ask questions to get Mark's interest.

He began to speak, and she focused her attention on him.

"I can't suggest strongly enough that you make immediate notes after each performance," he was saying. "That's the only way to keep the performances clear in your mind."

Heads bobbed in agreement.

"Now, any questions before the next part begins?"

"Yes." One of the male students inched forward. "Is this the kind of music you were talking about?"

Mark nodded. "Yes. One thing to remember is that this opera actually began in the streets. Streets are noisy places. That accounts, in part, for the piercing quality of the music. These were itinerant players. On the street you must attract your audience before you can even play to them."

One of the woman students spoke hesitantly, and looked to her companion for support. "I thought it seemed as though each actor had a kind of music of his own that went with him."

"Very good, Miss Donovan. You have sharp ears. Quite often each character has his own leitmotif."

"Like the Wagnerian opera," added her companion, and Claudia found herself digging her nails into her palms as Mark smiled at the two young women. Jealous! She was jealous of Mark, she thought, and turned partially away from Dell to shield her face. Things were getting worse and worse.

The high-pitched music began again. "Notice the different ways the male and female actors move," he suggested. "Each gesture, look, step portrays the character's sex, age, and personality. Watch the smiles. There are twenty different ways of smiling."

Claudia turned away, back toward the cleared circle where a pale-faced young maiden with pink tint spreading upward from her cheekbones to her eyes came gliding forth in small, dainty steps, each foot barely separated from the one behind it. Her shining belted robe of satin was resplendent with gold and silver embroidered dragons, and as she moved forward in her slow, clearly feminine walk, she raised a long cascading sleeve and giggled behind it. Behind her bounced the *chou*, the clown, a patch of white paint outlined in black around his eyes and nose, his silk robe liberally covered with the patches that denoted his poverty.

Claudia sighed. Here was true artistry. The simple flicker of an eyelid, the tilt of the head, the movement of one delicate finger—and woman personified stood before her.

After the performance of this troupe, Mark led them through various byways to where another troupe was performing. Morning moved into afternoon as they sampled exotic foods from the traveling vendors.

It was late afternoon when they once more neared the hotel, and not once had Claudia spoken to Mark. Several times his eyes had passed over her as he talked to the class, but they held no special recognition. It was almost as though yesterday had never happened.

"What are you doing tonight?" asked Dell as they entered the lobby and the group began to disband. "Want to paint the town with me?"

"Sorry." Her reply came automatically. Much as she might hide behind Dell in the daytime, she had no desire to spend an evening with him. Especially not painting the town. "I have other plans."

Dell nodded. "I supposed you would. But I had to ask. You're an eternal challenge to me. Well, have fun washing your hair." And he crossed to the entrance to the bar.

Claudia stared after him. Obnoxious as he could be at times, it was hard to stay angry with Dell. She felt suddenly tired, exhausted by their day's excursions. A quick glance around showed her that Mark was not in sight and she headed for the elevator.

6

Though she had fully intended to go to her room and relax once she reached it, Claudia found it impossible to be still. She sat down, got up, rearranged the things in her suitcase, and sat down again. She tried reviewing her notes. She tried studying her guidebook. She even tried outlining a paper on the origins of the theater in Southeast Asia, a paper she would never have to write.

Finally she pulled off her clothes and went into the shower. But the warm water falling on her body was anything but soothing. Every drop seemed to remind her of the touch of Mark's hands. How could she recall so vividly something that had happened so long ago? Why hadn't the memory faded? It seemed to be even brighter than when she had laid it to rest—or thought she had—in the depths of her unconscious.

She made the shower a quick one, since it certainly wasn't having the desired effect, and toweled herself dry. That, too, was distracting. Her body didn't seem to be the familiar thing she had known for so long. It was full of aches and longings, yearnings and desires more suitable to a sex-conscious teenager than a mature woman who had decided that men had no permanent place in her life.

Back in the small bedroom, she pulled down the spread. She just needed a good night's sleep. Jet lag was taking its toll. She would just lie there calmly and drift off to sleep. That was the thing to do.

But it was much easier to decide what to do than actually to do it. Sleep had never been further from her than it was as she lay there in the semidarkness of the strange hotel room. She tried all the relaxation techniques she had ever heard or read about, but none of them worked.

Her nightgown, short as it was, tangled about her as she tossed and turned, trying to find a position of comfort. But nothing did any good. Finally, in exasperation, she threw back the covers and sat up.

A glance at her watch showed it was ten o'clock. She sighed. If only she had something to read. A paperback mystery, maybe. Something to engage her mind, to keep thoughts of Mark Hanson at bay, at least temporarily.

She made a quick decision. She would dress and go down to the lobby. The gift shop had paperbacks. She could pick up something there, maybe even go into the bar for a nightcap. She drank very seldom, but tonight seemed to call for strong measures. She couldn't go through the whole trip without sleeping.

She pulled a soft dress from her suitcase and shook it out. She didn't know why she should choose to wear a dress on a simple errand to the gift shop, but she didn't stop to examine her motives. She slipped into her bra and panties, pulled on a half-slip, stepped into her sandals, and slid the dress over her head.

It was a simply cut dress of pale blue, made of one of the new wrinkle-free fabrics, and it clung to her body in a way she did not remember it having done the day she bought it. She brushed her hair briskly. This new awareness of her body—or perhaps she should think of it as "renewed," since it brought back so vividly those feelings she had known with Mark on that memorable weekend—was very disconcerting. It was almost as though an old, reliable friend had suddenly changed, taken on new and startling dimensions. She could never be sure now of how it would react.

She picked up her purse and room key. She was going to get something to keep her mind off Mark Hanson. He had interfered with her life for the last time. She was determined not to let it happen again.

The lobby was still brilliantly lit, the gift shop doing a thriving business. Checking the sign on the door, she saw that it was open twenty-four hours a day and decided to have her drink first. Maybe if she sat in a secluded corner and quietly looked around, she could distract her mind, keep it from so often presenting her with feelings and memories that she was better off without.

She took her screwdriver to a little booth and nursed it slowly. One should be plenty, she told herself. Because she so seldom drank the stuff, its effect on her could be rather dramatic. She stirred the drink slowly, staring down into its orange depths, the bar and its environs slipping from her conciousness as, her resolution brushed aside, her mind again reverted to her memories.

"Penny for your thoughts," said a deep voice.

The stirrer fell from her fingers as she looked up to meet Mark Hanson's eyes. "Not . . . worth it," she replied, grateful that the dim lighting concealed the flush that was rising to her cheeks.

He gestured to the empty seat across from her. "Mind if I join you?"

"I . . . I . . . No, of course not." She was so flustered, she couldn't think of a reasonable excuse. She had barely touched her drink; she couldn't just run away because he had showed up.

"Having trouble getting to sleep?" he asked as he slid into the seat.

She nodded. "Jet lag, I guess."

He smiled sympathetically. "It affects us all differently. I was having trouble too. Anyway, the evening is still young. I imagine a lot of your colleagues are out enjoying themselves."

"A city's nightlife always seems tourist-oriented to me," she said. "I prefer looking at the more ordinary manifestations of a city's culture." That sounded much more sober and pedantic than she felt, but it was better than dissolving into helpless giggles as some girlish part of her wanted to do.

Mark nodded soberly. "I'm very much in agreement with that," he replied. "But the city does have some beauties that can only be seen at night. For instance, partway up Mount Faber, on Kampong

Bahru Road to the west of the city, there's a fabulous view at night. All the lights of the city and the harbor. It's really outstanding with the reflections on the water and all."

"I imagine it is. I think I saw it described in the literature somewhere. 'Like a necklace of diamonds,' or something like that."

Mark chuckled. "I have to admit that I'm not much of a metaphor maker. Not that I don't admire a good one," he hastened to add, then smiled sheepishly. "I'm certainly aware that your hero, Shakespeare, was very good in that department. But I've never aspired to be a writer."

"Or an actor?" The question came out of nowhere and surprised her.

He grinned. "Sorry to disappoint you, but I'm not a frustrated actor either. I'm just a scholar. I like to study new and different things."

"Me too." She didn't know why she said that. For several years now she had thought of nothing but Edmund Kean and her course work.

"Really?" He did not wait for an answer. "Tell me about your dissertation. Since it's about Kean, I can guess which side of the nature-versus-art controversy you're on."

Claudia smiled. "I can't help it. It just seems to make more sense. Nature is the way things *are*. To make natural things into art is to deprive them of their life. I don't see how anyone can prefer the artificial to the real."

He nodded thoughtfully. "As you're aware, of course, this theater we're studying is art. Everything is stylized, ritualized. Ritualized is a good word, incidentally, since much of the stuff has religious beginnings. But in answer to your argument, proponents of art would say that it actually is *more* real than reality. That the classic gestures and movements have more meaning for humankind than one man's interpretation."

"Of course I've heard that kind of reasoning," Claudia said. "But it fails to explain how the classic forms were arrived at in the first place. Unless you want to believe in fiats handed down from the gods, these forms, too, must have been originated by men."

Mark smiled ruefully. "You're a sharp debater, Claudia. I don't have an answer to that. I can only repeat what some people said, even in Kean's time. It is possible to enjoy both kinds of performances. Perhaps nature and art both have their place in the drama. Perhaps it would be noticeably poorer if either of them was missing."

She considered this thoughtfully for a moment, then smiled slightly. "Well, that's the best argument you've advanced so far."

He chuckled and indicated her glass. "Can I get you another drink?"

To her surprise, she realized that her glass was empty. "No. No thanks. I'm not much of a drinker. But have another yourself if you like." Belatedly she saw the invitation implied in this.

"I'd rather take a drive up Mount Faber and look at the lights. Will you come with me?"

Yearning hit her with a terrible impact. During their conversation, she had been mostly conscious of his mind, of the stimulation of exchanging ideas. Though his physical presence had been pulling on her senses, that pressure had been subdued, felt only lightly. But with this invitation, her body had come instantly alive. "I . . ." She hesitated. She wanted very much to go with him, but after last night's kiss she was not sure she should chance it.

He reached across the little table to cover her hand with his, and her nerve endings quivered. "Please, Claudia. It's a shame to miss the view. It's one of the most beautiful in the whole city."

She glanced at her watch and he caught the gesture. "I promise not to keep you out late."

His eyes seemed full of a yearning that matched her own, and when he turned her hand over and began to lightly trace the lines in her palm, she capitulated. "All right, if you promise."

What she should have asked for, she told herself as she followed him outside to the rented car, was a promise not to repeat last night's kiss. But she could not ask for that, of course. The asking would be tantamount to inviting another. And, much as her body might desire such a thing, her mind was full of warning bells that could not be ignored.

As he eased the car out onto the road, Claudia tried to lean back in the seat. It would do no good to sit like a board with her hands clasped so tightly in her lap.

"I take it you've been here often," she said, trying to find a safe topic of conversation.

Mark nodded. "Yes. Singapore's an interesting place. Many cultures living side by side. And doing a pretty good job of it, too. The U.S. isn't the only melting pot around."

Claudia nodded.

For some moments they were silent. Gradually the brightly lit streets fell behind them and the car began to climb a winding road. Masses of tropical shrubs clustered around houses that seemed to be almost part of the mountain.

The heavy fragrance drifted in through the open car windows. Claudia inhaled: "Mmmm, the flowers smell good."

"This is good flower country," he said. "Jasmine, bougainvillea, magnolias."

Claudia inhaled again. "Their fragrance is awfully sweet. Too much of that might be hard to handle."

Mark shrugged. "The tropics are like that. Life is profuse and vibrant. In many instances, it's also very short, but quite intense."

She considered this. "It's almost as though the intensity makes up for the shortness."

Mark nodded. "The classic question is: Would you prefer a long dull life or a short exciting one?"

She sighed. "A loaded question if I ever heard one."

He gave her a sharp glance before returning his eyes to the road. "But I'm still interested in your answer."

She shook her head. "A question like that needs thought. I can't just answer it off the top of my head."

"That would probably be the truer response," he replied, as he guided the car around another curve.

"Why?" Her curiosity was piqued.

"Because then you wouldn't have time to be sensible about it."

Her laugh was almost rueful. "I'm afraid I'm always sensible. So I suppose the long dull life would be my choice."

The sound he made was unintelligible, but when she turned to ask him to repeat what he'd said, his face wore such a strange expression that she did not dare.

And then the realization hit her. He was thinking of that weekend they had spent together—that insane, wonderful weekend.

"Of course," she chattered on, her tension mounting, "it all depends on what one considers dull. A long life of scholarship might be dull to some, yet exciting to others."

He nodded. "Yes, that's true. But here we are." And he swung the car off the road.

Moonlight showed her a small paved area beside the road. To one side a path led through a tangle of flowering shrubs. Beyond that she couldn't see.

He went around the car and opened her door, extending his hand to help her out. She hesitated for a fraction of a second, but avoiding his help could be worse than taking it, so she put her hand in his. His fingers were warm and strong. She wanted to cling to them, to keep on touching him. But as soon as she was out of the car, she eased her fingers from his.

"You can really smell the flowers here," he said. "But wait till you see the city."

He took her by the elbow and led her toward the narrow path. "Take it easy here," he cautioned, shifting his grip momentarily to her fingers and giving them a quick squeeze. "Things grow fast. We don't want a branch to snag that lovely dress." And he stepped into the path in front of her.

The quick color rushed to her face again as she realized that she had probably put this dress on hoping that somehow she would see Mark. Why else would she have chosen a dress just to go down to the gift shop? She'd certainly had no intention of trying to attract a strange man. Mark Hanson was already more than she could handle.

Mark emerged on the other side of the shrubbery and turned to face her. In the moonlight his eyes glittered with anticipation. That was the first thing she saw. Then, with a grand gesture, he stepped to one side and indicated the view beyond him.

"Oh, Mark!" For the moment she forgot everything but the splendor spread out before her. Now she could see why people liked to build up here. Imagine having a view like this from your living room window.

"So it's worth the ride," he said quietly as they stood side by side.

"Oh yes. It's much better than a diamond necklace. It's . . . it's . . ."

"Alive?" he suggested gently.

"Yes, that's it. It reminds me of that French theologian, Teilhard de Chardin, when he talks about the lights of a city, the energy—he means human, spiritual energy, I think—that hangs in the air above a city. Oh, Mark." She turned eagerly toward him, unaware that for the second time in as many minutes she had used his Christian name. "I can't thank you enough for bringing me up here. Seeing this was worth . . ."

Her voice faltered. When she swung toward him, she discovered he was not looking at the view but at her. Mysterious shadows veiled his dark eyes as a cloud drifted over the moon. But there was no mistaking the feel of his hands on her arms, drawing her close against him. Within the shelter of his arms, her cheek against his shoulder, she stood silent. It was this that her body had been needing—the simple touch of his.

Except, of course, that it was not really simple. The longer she stood there with his arms around her, with her body against his, the stronger grew her desire.

Once they had been one. And the memory of that experience had never left her. It was a memory that could not be erased.

Her pulse began to pound in her throat, her hands grew clammy, and her knees quaked. Warning bells clanged in her mind. This was insanity. She must stop it. But her body refused to move. If anything, her desire mounted. She had denied her feelings for so long that they had accumulated great power. She just could not move away from him after all those years of need and longing. Not when she was at last where she had wanted to be.

She tried to think, to marshal logical arguments against her feelings, but she could not. They were far too strong to be intimidated by mere logic.

She felt his hand move away from her waist. His fingers traced the outline of her cheek, down to the point of her chin, where they stopped. His grip was gentle but firm as he tipped her face upward toward his.

She tried to remain cold, rigid. But her body would not listen to her mind. It trembled with eagerness. She clutched the skirt of her dress in an effort to keep her hands from creeping up around his neck, and pressed her lips together tightly.

He did not attempt to force them open. His kiss was gentle and persuasive. Softly, tenderly, his lips caressed hers until, in spite of all she could do, they softened and opened for him. Her body ceased to resist the pressure of his hand on her back, and she melted against him willingly, all thought of caution, of danger, buried in the avalanche of emotion that rioted through her. She might tell herself that she was a mature, sensible woman, no longer susceptible to the feelings that had once overwhelmed a naive teenager, but the truth of the matter was something far different.

The feelings which Mark had wakened in her so long ago, feelings which she had then buried in her unconscious, were no longer those of a young girl. But, because of that very fact, and because she had suppressed and ignored them all these years, the desires of her body were far stronger, infinitely more powerful, than they had been at first. She was shaken to the very core of her being by their intensity.

He released her mouth but kept her body close against his. "Look at the city now," he whispered.

Obediently she turned her head till his chin touched her temple and together they stood looking down at the glowing lights. Sudden tears blinded her eyes, making them a shimmering, shifting scene of great beauty. But she was far too conscious of herself and her feelings to be able to truly appreciate it. She tried to think, tried to find a safe topic of conversation. "I . . . The street opera was fascinating," she blurted out, and wondered suddenly if he would laugh at this too obvious change of subject.

But his voice remained soft and gentle. "Yes, it is. One of my favorite genres. But let's not talk now. Let's just enjoy the view."

Such a reasonable request could hardly be ignored, and she remained silent, gazing out over the shimmering city. But it was not the beauty of the scene before her that kept the tears in her eyes and the lump in her throat; she truly did not see the city at all. Her mind was in the grip of memory, and her tear-laden eyes saw only pictures of the past: A laughing young girl, hand in hand with a handsome man, her face turned adoringly toward his. Their two figures on the bed, two naked figures engrossed in each other, entwined in the embraces of love.

Deep within her, desire pulsed and pounded, and her body quivered there in his arms as the figures in her mind collapsed into contentment. The pain of his leaving had been great; she had admitted that long ago. And she had decided then that it was too high a price to pay for even that ecstatic pleasure. But that decision had been made alone and abandoned, in the dark night of her solitary bed. Not when the man she desired was standing next to her, his arms around her, his body close to hers.

Desire flamed through her, igniting every nerve, every skin cell. She could feel every breath he took, every swallow, every sigh. She was attuned to him, only him. The night around them faded; the lovely view, the warm air, the pervasive scent of flowers—all vanished as her senses reported only what had to do with him.

Under her cheek she felt the smooth weave of his tropical suit. She inhaled the clean male scent of him, the tang of aftershave and soap. The thought took form slowly but insistently. If she turned her face just a little . . . and raised herself on her tiptoes . . . her mouth would find his. And if it did . . .

She struggled with the feelings sweeping through her. Except for that one wild weekend, her whole life had been ordered and sane. But the impact of that weekend could not be denied. Not while she stood there beside the man who had literally changed her whole life. She should have refused his invitation to drive up to see the view. She had known it at the time. But she had so wanted to be with him, to experience that joy in living that being with him meant. And now . . .

She could not help herself. Still within the circle of his arms, she began to turn toward him.

"Claudia."

She felt his breath against her lips, and then his mouth, soft, persuasive, and she gave up all attempts to hold herself back.

When he released her mouth some time later, her whole body was trembling. Without a word, he took her hand and led her back to the car.

The drive back down the mountain was made in silence. She could think of nothing but the response of her body to his kisses, of how much she still wanted him.

The mountain road became the brightly lit city street and still they remained silent. She could think of nothing to say that wouldn't sound stupid, and he was equally quiet.

As he pulled into the parking lot, he finally spoke. "I'll see you up to your room."

She understood now what they meant by saying someone's heart leaped up in their throat. She could scarcely breathe as they crossed the parking lot and entered the lobby. Moments later they stood outside her door.

She stared up into his eyes, willing her own to hide her secret feelings. "I . . . enjoyed the ride." She forced her suddenly dry lips to form the innocuous words. "Thank you."

He took one step toward her and she thought that he would kiss her again. But he stopped suddenly, with still a foot of space between them.

"Claudia." He seemed to be struggling with words, and she tried to remain calm, to remind herself that she must tell him no, that that was the only sensible thing to do.

"Good night," he whispered. "And thank you."

He turned swiftly and was gone, disappearing around the corner of the hall without looking back.

Slowly she opened the door and went into her room, unsure whether she felt relief or disappointment, aware finally that she felt both.

7

Claudia, settling into a seat at the School of Dance in Bangkok, sighed. Jetting from place to place might seem like fun to some people, perhaps even to her under other circumstances. But she was not sleeping well, and that, added to the stress of trying to behave as though Mark Hanson were nothing more than a teacher, was wearing her out.

Her mind slipped back to the mixup at the hotel that morning. For some reason, the hotel had reserved one room too few. Mark had handled it well, she thought, simply telling the group that he would register at another one nearby.

She examined the feelings of disappointment that had swamped her at his announcement, feelings that she had pushed to the back of her mind at the time. It wasn't difficult to figure out why she felt as she did. If Mark wasn't staying in the same hotel, she was not at all likely to run into him in the lobby again. She recognized now that she had been hoping to do exactly that.

If only she had listened to the part of her mind that had counseled common sense. Anyone should know not to touch the fire that had already burned them once, said that part of her mind scornfully.

But when the fire was so beautiful, retorted another part, and the warmth it gave so full of joy, no one could be blamed for hoping to tame it, to have it always there.

She was pulled away from this fanciful thinking and back into reality by the sound of Mark's voice drifting softly out over the group. "Thai drama is dance drama," he was saying. "Students enrolling here must be younger than thirteen. The training is long—six years in preliminary courses alone."

Claudia looked out at the slim, supple little girls. They seemed so very young to be embarking on such arduous careers. And yet she knew that the theater demanded great sacrifices of hard work and training from all its participants.

"There are four role categories," Mark's voice continued. She was glad she couldn't see him. That made it easier for her to concentrate on the sense of his words and not the sight of him. "Demons and monkeys are played by men. Human roles, male and female, generally by women. A student is assigned to one category and remains in it, perfecting his or her art until every step, every gesture, becomes second nature."

As the tones of a xylophone echoed softly in her ears, Claudia watched the little girls. They moved in formation, feet, hands, head and torso undulating in unison to the rhythms of the music. They seemed perfection to her, but the teacher moved among them, adjusting an arm or hand, moving a foot slightly.

The next group they stopped to watch was composed of small boys, their scarlet breeches and white tops making vibrant splashes of color.

"These boys are training for the monkey role," Mark told them. "They must learn many kinds of acrobatics."

Claudia held her breath as the instructor moved down the line, helping each small boy with a flying somersault. They seemed so small, these boys. At home they would be digging worms to go fishing, engrossed in sandlot baseball, or just looking for mischief. But the faces of these children were deadly serious.

Mark led the class to where another line of boys practiced together. Here an instructor with a small bamboo baton beat out the time as the scarlet-clad legs turned, sidestepped, advanced, and retreated, all in perfect unison. "These will be demons," Mark explained. "Their roles, too, require acrobatic finesse and are very demanding."

Later, when the tour was finished, Mark looked out over the assembled group. "The Thai drama descended from old court drama," he began.

Claudia, conscious of his eyes, endeavored to still the clamoring of her body and listen to his words. There was no point in trying to figure out what he was thinking or feeling. In brutal fact, last evening might not have meant anything important to him. It might have been nothing more than a pleasant way to spend some free time. That was the way she ought to be thinking about it herself. She brought her attention back to his words.

". . . founded in 1934," Mark was saying. "It's called the School of Sangkhit. 'Sangita'—the Sanscrit word from which 'sangkhit' is derived—means dance, dramatic expression, and music, all in one word."

He smiled and Claudia's heart leaped. But it was not the smile of a lover, only that of a teacher, and it was not directed at her.

"I suggest you split up and watch what interests you most. The teachers here will be glad to help you with any questions you may have."

His eyes slid over her face, but there was no special recognition in them. They did not reflect any feeling at all. She sighed and turned away from the group. The little boys had been interesting to watch, but it was the smooth flowing motions of the little girls that fascinated her most, and she made her way back to that room.

As she stood watching, lost in the beauty of the movements, she was joined by a smiling young teacher. "You are interested in our dance."

Claudia nodded. "They make it look so easy, but I understand they study for many years."

"That is so. Eleven for the most advanced students. Did Mark tell you much about our dances?"

Claudia pressed her suddenly trembling hands against her sides. "I understand they were originally court dances." She managed to get the words out without stammering. Of course Mark knew people here. This was his territory. That's why he was leading the class. But the thought that he knew this smooth-cheeked, smiling young woman in her exotic clothes, knew her well enough that she should call him Mark, made Claudia ache somewhere deep inside. She pulled her mind away from her feelings and groped for words. "Can you tell me more?"

"Yes. Of course. Our dance is originally descended from the Indian. Our classical dances—which is what we teach here—each tell a story from the Ramayana, the famous Indian epic. There are also folk dances." The lovely nose wrinkled slightly in distaste. "We do not, of course, teach those."

"Of course," Claudia found herself echoing.

"The children spend six years learning the fundamentals, three years in the intermediary class. Only the best go on for the last two years of advanced training. This costume which you see me wearing . . ." She indicated her silver and gold brocaded robe with its long flowing sash and narrow skirt. "This is the traditional costume. Usually we also wear a conical headdress."

Claudia nodded, remembering the pictures in her guidebook. "Have you a puppet theater here?" she asked, pushing aside the question she would have liked most to ask—how well did this young woman know Mark?

"We did. Though today it is rarely performed. Our *nang,* or shadow play, is thought to be one of the three old forms which contributed to our drama. I can tell you something—"

"So this is where you're hiding out." Dell's entrance was anything but quiet, and several little girls were so startled by his voice that they faltered.

Claudia turned to him. "Sssh," she remonstrated. "You're disturbing the practice."

The teacher's smooth face gave no hint of irritation, but her eyes flickered toward her charges. "If you'll excuse me . . ."

"Of course. I understand." Claudia tried by her tone and expression to convey her regret. Dell could be such a blundering idiot. Though why she should feel responsible for him she couldn't understand. "Come on," she said in exasperation. "We'll talk outside."

Later that evening, sitting beside Dell in the dining room of the Sala Norasingh, the theater-restaurant where Mark had taken them to eat and to observe a performance of classical dance, Claudia tried to organize her chaotic thoughts. The day had not gone well.

It was annoying, now that she was genuinely interested in this drama, to have Dell dogging her heels. But to send him packing would destroy the only defense she had against Mark. And so she was more or less forced to put up with his company, irritating as it might be.

He looked down at his plate and grimaced. "They must have cast-iron stomachs here."

Determined not to let him spoil her evening, Claudia forced a chuckle. "You shouldn't have said you wanted the hot dinner. Mine is mild and it still makes my eyes water." She smiled at him. "What happened to the culture vulture? Just think what tales you'll have to tell Papa."

Dell managed a smile. "If I reach home intact."

She grinned at him good-naturedly. "Oh, just shut up and eat." She turned back toward her own plate, where a spicy chicken and mushroom stew with an unpronounceable name awaited her.

She managed the stew without too many refills of her water glass, but a glance at Dell's dinner, served exotically on a banana leaf, made her glad she had chosen the milder dish. If his fish in hot sauce was as hot as he said it was, she would never have been able to finish it. And an empty stomach would be no help in getting to sleep tonight. She had enough trouble with that as it was.

The plates around her were gradually emptying and people turned expectant faces toward the stage. Claudia, conscious of Mark's presence across the table to her left, pointedly refrained from looking in that direction. She knew he was flanked by two female students; knew, too, that they were probably bombarding him with questions. Well, that was one of the tried and true ways of gaining the prof's attention.

The waiter appeared at her side and offered her a plate of sticky-looking candies. As she reached for one, Mark turned toward the student at his left. Over her shoulder his eyes met Claudia's. The flicker of warmth was momentary, vanishing almost as soon as she glimpsed it. Shaken nevertheless by its intensity, she dropped her gaze to the plate before her and, unseeing, selected a sweetmeat.

It was even stickier than it had looked, and she popped it into her mouth, setting her mind to analyzing the ingredients as a way of calming herself. She recognized the taste and texture of coconut and rice, but she could not put names to the subtle spices that flavored it. The effort, however, helped to restore her senses and she was able to turn once more toward the stage where the rising curtain and silvery tones of a xylophone announced the beginning of the dance.

She leaned forward in her seat, eager to see this performance that would reflect the skills acquired at the school. This would be a finished performance, the culmination of all those years of hard work.

As the dancers began their soft stylized movements, a deep sigh welled up from within her. This was art in its best sense, she told herself. Stylized, ritualized, yes. But also very beautiful. Had Kemble been able to put grace and finesse into his performances instead of the theatrical bombast the reviewers had so often accused him of, that battle between nature and art might have turned out very differently.

She turned to whisper her observation to Dell, then stopped. He would not even know that John Kemble had been the most highly regarded Shakespearian actor on the early-nineteenth-century stage until Edmund Kean's genius had lifted him to peaks of excellence that Kemble had never dreamed of.

Claudia sighed. To share her thoughts with Dell would mean a long, involved explanation. For all his gibes about being a culture vulture, Dell was a student of the American theater only, a tried and true jingoist. She smiled to herself as the little-used word popped into her mind. Yet it was the right word. Dell was so violently nationalistic that he could scarcely even see the beauties of Shakespearian drama. And surely anyone— She laughed at herself then. If Dell was a jingoist, she herself, with her exceptionally strong love for things British, came perilously close to being an anglophile.

Well, she thought, startled out of her reflections as a demon came somersaulting onto the stage, she was at least learning.

Beside her, Dell heaved a sigh of martyrdom. Fortunately it was drowned out by the music, now growing more ferocious as monkeys and demons tumbled about on the stage. She turned and whispered, "Cheer up. You'll live."

He gave her such a bright smile that for a moment she wondered if he'd mistaken what she'd said. But when she felt his arm slide possessively around her shoulders and heard him whisper, "You could cheer me up," she realized that his martyrdom had a purpose. He meant to use it to get sympathy from her.

She turned again, ready to tell him it wouldn't work, and from across the table Mark's eyes bored into hers. She could not read the expression in them. When she tried, they went dull and lifeless—cold, hard shields that kept her out.

Her face flamed and she felt as though she had done him some terrible wrong. She was behaving stupidly, said one part of her mind. She certainly wasn't responsible for Mark Hanson's feelings. And anyway, when had he given much consideration to hers?

This was her chance, said that part of her mind. Let him think that there really was something between her and Dell. But she found the thought so disturbing that she moved automatically to ease out from under his arm.

Dell grinned and shrugged. "Nothing ventured, nothing gained," he quoted as he withdrew his arm and focused his attention once more on the stage.

Some time later, showered and in bed, Claudia relived the day. That lovely girl at the school knew Mark. That lovely girl with the smooth ivory skin and glossy black hair, with the deep mysterious eyes fringed by long, dark lashes, and with the supple, lithe body of a dancer. How *well* did she know him?

The question haunted her, but of course she had no way of answering it. Was he with that girl now? The thought sent her sitting bolt upright. Would he take her dancing or would he just . . .

With an exclamation of disgust, Claudia threw aside the covers and leaped to her feet. She certainly didn't intend to spend another night lying awake because of Mark Hanson. She cursed softly. If only she had that mystery she had meant to buy last night. Anything to divert her mind.

She glanced at her watch. It was close to midnight. She had to get some sleep. Maybe she should get dressed and go after a book. Maybe she should have a nightcap at the bar. That would relax her.

But Mark wasn't staying at this hotel, said the voice in her head. So even if he weren't with that woman, he wasn't likely to be in the bar here.

She paced the room nervously, the short sheer nightie that had been a last-minute whim fluttering against her body like tender, gentle caresses. With another curse she threw herself on her stomach on the bed and began to pound the pillow. She had to stop this kind of childishness. She was a grown woman— mature, capable, independent. She didn't need any man. And most of all, she didn't need Mark Hanson.

With a sigh, she turned over. She might as well try to read something about Thailand. Tomorrow was their free day here and she could expect to spend it alone. But she didn't intend to sit moping in this hotel.

She sat up and began pushing the pillows into shape. If she didn't get her normal amount of sleep tonight, it was not going to be the end of the world.

Satisfied with the pillows, she reached out for her guidebook but jumped as the phone shrilled. Her hand trembled in midair as she remained frozen. Who could be calling her this late? Dell had seemed to take her no as definite. Probably it was a wrong number.

Unable to wait any longer, she picked up the phone. "Hello."

"Claudia."

Her whole body began to tremble at the sound of Mark's voice. "Y-yes?"

"I hope I didn't wake you."

"No. I wasn't sleeping yet." She was glad her voice seemed steadier than her shaking body.

"Good."

There was a longish pause, and she swallowed hastily and tried to organize her thoughts, wondering what she should say.

"I . . . I'm downstairs."

In disbelief she heard the nervousness in his voice.

"I . . . I want to see you. Will you come down and have a drink with me?"

"I . . . The others . . ." she stammered. "You're not staying here."

"We can go to my hotel's bar. It isn't far." As she hesitated, he hurried on. "Please, Claudia. I really need to talk to you."

She could not resist the pleading in his voice, even when the saner part of her mind scolded that she was being a fool. So he needed. What about *her* needs?

"Please, Claudia," he begged.

And, knowing that she shouldn't, she capitulated. "It'll take me a few minutes. I . . . I'm not dressed."

"Take your time." His voice was calm now that he knew she was coming. "I'll be waiting in the lobby."

"Okay."

8

~∞∞∞∞∞∞∞∞∞∞∞∞∞~

Half an hour later they were sitting in a booth in a dark corner of the bar of Mark's hotel. Absently, Claudia stirred her screwdriver. Her heart was still pounding under her blue dress. She could not wipe from her mind the look of joy that had leaped into his face as she stepped from the elevator. Her bare elbow could still feel the pressure of his guiding fingers. Yet on the way he had hardly spoken a word to her.

He regarded her across the little table, his dark eyes serious. "Thank you for coming," he said. "I . . ." He shook his head. "I hardly know how to say this."

She sat, silent, her hands twisting in her lap. Unsure of what he was trying to tell her, she didn't know how to respond to him.

He ran a hand through his unruly dark hair. "I guess the best thing to do is just to plunge in."

"I guess so." She wished her voice sounded stronger.

"I . . . I'm so pleased you came on this trip. When you came to my office that day . . ." He picked up his drink and took a quick swallow. "My life took on new dimensions." His eyes met hers and they were open now, open and vulnerable.

"After the . . . accident I lost all joy in life. Nothing seemed to matter much without my family." He sighed deeply. "Except my work, and that was painful. So full of memories of them."

Her heart ached at the pain on his face even while she rebelled at being forced to see how much he had loved that other woman.

"But those that are left must go on living. I've seen that more clearly these last few days. She would not expect me to forsake life, to reject my chance at joy, at happiness."

Her trembling slowed a little as she tried to understand these very private thoughts he was revealing to her.

"Seeing you again . . ." He smiled. "Makes me feel young. Young and carefree. Thinking only of the moment."

She bit her lip to keep back a sharp reply. So that had been his reasoning. It hurt, but she supposed it made sense. To him, at least.

"I want to regain some of the joy we shared that weekend long ago," he went on. "I remember it so vividly. So beautifully."

His eyes darkened with desire and she felt the response of her body.

"We share so much," he went on, his voice warm

and persuasive. "Our love of the theater for one thing." He smiled sheepishly. "Even if we do study different kinds. And our love of learning in general."

He paused and looked down at his drink while she waited, her heart pounding even harder.

He raised his eyes again and met hers. His smile was boyish and rueful. "I guess I'm taking the long way around because I'm afraid of being rejected." He straightened his shoulders and took a deep breath. "Claudia, I want us to share our bodies. There, I've said it. Will you come up to my room with me? Please?"

She heard all the warnings, all the intimations of pain to come that her mind issued. It was clear to her that she should refuse. But she knew, too, that she would not. She could not turn away from Mark, from the obvious need in his eyes. And, to be quite honest with herself, she could not deny her own insistent need.

"Yes," she said softly. "Yes, Mark. I'll go with you."

After that, none of it seemed real. They left their drinks practically untouched and, oblivious to everything but the urgency of their need for each other, made their way to his room.

She could hardly believe this was happening, though she recognized with belated awareness that part of her had been hoping for exactly this since the moment she'd first walked into his office. She might as well be honest with herself. She wanted him, wanted him very badly.

He unlocked the door and stood aside for her to enter. She stepped in and stopped, overcome with a momentary urge to flee. But he was between her and the hall, and besides, she really didn't want to leave him. Not now. Not so close to . . .

She heard the click as he locked the door. Then he came up behind her, his hands stealing around her, coming to rest under her breasts. She knew her heart was pounding, was sure he must be able to feel it.

"Claudia." His lips were near her ear. She felt the warmth of his body against her back. "Claudia, are you afraid of me?"

"No. I . . ."

He swung her around to face him, his eyes searching her face. He must have liked what he saw there for he crushed her to him. "Oh, Claudia."

She felt his body against hers, hard and demanding, and she wanted him. But she could find no words to tell him so. She raised her face to his, unconsciously lifting on her tiptoes to bring her mouth closer to his.

There was no need to do more. His lips found hers and the excitement that had been tingling in her whenever she looked at him swept uproariously through her veins. Let tomorrow go, she told herself. There was only the here and now. Only this terrible insistent need that beat in her body like the pounding of surf on sand. She was no more capable than the sand of moving away, of escaping the force of this elemental attack.

His tongue moved gently, curiously along the wet curve of her parted lips, and a tremulous sigh escaped them. She clung to him, her body melting into his.

After long, ecstatic moments, he released her mouth. "God, how I've been wanting you," he groaned against her hair.

She thought of the many times she'd felt his eyes on

her. She thought of that evening, of Dell's arm around her shoulders. She opened her mouth to tell him there was nothing between her and Dell, and closed it abruptly. That was no concern of Mark's. What he had asked for was this night. She was prepared to give him that, prepared to give him *only* that, because that was all he wanted.

"Come." His arm around her, he led her toward the bed. "Let's sit down." He matched his actions to his words, sinking down beside her. "It's been a long time," he said, his fingers gently tracing the curve of her jaw.

She nodded. "Yes, a long time." His face was close to hers. She could see the lines of pain etched in it, the trace of gray in the hair at his temples. He was no longer a young man, no longer the idol of a teenager's dreams. But in the face so near her own she saw the likeness of the young, gloriously alive man she had once known. The laugh lines were still there, too, curving out from around his dark eyes.

"Claudia." His voice was full of longing. "Touch me," he pleaded. "I . . . I'm not sure you're really here."

Laughter bubbled up from some hidden place within her, tinged with irony, perhaps, but laughter nevertheless. His tone of voice definitely destroyed her fantasy. Idols were always on top of things, always calm and collected. Above all, they were never reduced to pleading.

She raised a tentative hand to his face. It had been so long since she'd touched a man, really touched him, since she had wanted to. Her fingers moved softly along the line of his jaw, her sensitive fingertips reporting the smoothness of freshly shaved skin. "You shaved." The observation came from her without thought.

He raised a dark eyebrow. "The eternal optimist."

His hand caught hers, turned it so he could kiss her palm. She felt the tip of his tongue there. Desire made her shiver. She looked down at his bent head and raised her other hand to caress the exposed nape of his neck.

He lifted his head abruptly. "I suppose you know you're driving me crazy. I can hardly keep my eyes off you." He grinned. "I just hope I don't give myself away during a class meeting."

"You could have either Sue or Caroline. I'd be willing to bet on it." She was surprised at herself for making such a comment. But she seemed to have lost all her defenses, all her barriers. She just said what she was thinking. Unless, of course, it had to do with that long-ago weekend.

"Those two?" His eyes searched hers. "They're more nuisance than anything else." His hand raised hers to his lips again and the same shiver of desire pulsed through her. "I've been in this business long enough to know when someone wants a better grade than they deserve." He grinned. "They think they're taking out insurance policies."

She couldn't help smiling back at him. "Poor girls. They're going to be very disappointed." It crossed her mind that no one in the class would ever suspect where Claudia Carstairs was at that moment. "It's a good thing Dad put me down only to audit," she added.

"A very good thing," he agreed. "Because otherwise I have the feeling you wouldn't be here with me now."

He smoothed the hair back from her forehead. "You're really a stickler for the rules, aren't you?" she said.

"Rules were made to protect people. Yes, I guess I am."

He was looking at her so seriously. Suddenly some part of her recognized the humor in this and she burst into laughter. "I'm sorry," she gasped, seeing his look of bewilderment. "But . . . but . . . I don't think you asked me up here to discuss academic ethics. And . . . it just seems funny."

"It is funny," he agreed, his mouth stretching in a grin. "Very funny. So let's stop it. Let's forget the years between, Claudia. Let's forget what time has done to us. Let's go back to when everything was new and joyous. When life stretched on forever, and joy had no end."

"Yes," she whispered, indescribably moved. If only, she thought with a pang, if only she could forget the years between—the years of pain and loneliness.

Mark reached for the zipper on her dress. "I want to undress you," he said softly. "I want to go slowly, exploring every beautiful inch of you."

Her heart was pounding in her throat; it made speech impossible. He slid the zipper downward. Slowly his hands sought her shoulders, moved the material aside until her smooth flesh was exposed. He planted a kiss on her bare shoulder, left a little trail of them up to her chin. He slid the dress downward until it lay in a silken swath around her waist.

In one swift movement he was on his knees, pulling off her sandals. His hands sought her waist and she lifted her hips so he could slide off her dress and half-slip. Now she wore only her flimsy panties and a lacy wisp of a bra.

She flushed as she wondered what he was thinking about such lingerie. She had been able to ignore men, to keep them on the boundaries of her life. To make that easier she had chosen plain, practical clothes. But she had been unable to give up her pretty lingerie. It was, after all, strictly for her eyes. Yet now, flushed and heady with the adoration on his face, she couldn't help wondering if there had been some other reason. Had some faint hope of seeing him again persisted in spite of all her efforts to eradicate it, and influenced her decision to wear underclothes so unlike the image she projected to the world?

"Claudia." His voice was hoarse as he fumbled with his buttons and shrugged out of his shirt. His trousers hit the floor with a soft, evocative sound, and he stepped out of them, and out of his sandals. Wearing only his shorts, he approached her.

Some instinct, or perhaps only her need, made her rise to meet him. She wanted to feel the whole length of him against her. His arms went around her and she sighed with pleasure at the good feel of him. His hands caressed her bare back, then moved downward toward the soft panties, unhooking her bra in the process. She could feel the warmth of his body, the crisp texture of his chest hair against her breasts.

Slowly, easily, his fingers slid inside her panties and peeled them down over her hips. Then they moved back up, to release her breasts from their lacy confinement.

Her body seemed to be on fire. All the pent-up need of the long years was clamoring to be released. She

THIS BRIEF INTERLUDE

watched breathlessly as he dropped his shorts to the floor; then he took her hand and led her to the bed.

He threw back the covers and, turning to her, scooped her up suddenly into his arms. "Remember?" he whispered. "Remember how it was?"

The sudden tears blinded her, but she managed to answer him. "Yes, yes. I remember." And she buried her face in his chest, just as she had done so long ago. And, as he had then, he laid her gently on the bed and joined her there.

With him there beside her in the bed, the pain of the old memories was gone, eclipsed by the joy of the moment. The pain that she had felt, the pain she might feel again when this brief interlude was over—neither mattered in the face of the joy she was feeling then.

She gave herself up to that joy, to the wonderful touch of his hands and mouth, that touch that wakened all her senses, that made her wholly and completely female. His mouth moved over her exultant body, nibbling on an earlobe, caressing an erect nipple, leaving a trail of wet kisses across her flat stomach, down the sensitive skin of her thighs.

She moaned, hardly knowing that she did so. Her memories had been vivid, but overlaid with so much pain. This, the reality, was unimaginably better than those memories. Her body moved in response to his kiss, his touch. He was building desire in her. Like a coiled spring, it wound tighter and tighter with each caress, each kiss, until she felt ready to explode with pent-up longing.

Reaching for his shoulders, she tried to draw his body up on hers. It was torture to be separated from him.

He slid lightly up the length of her. She sighed as

she felt his weight, the good pressure of his body against hers. She wrapped her arms around his neck and pulled his head down toward hers. She wanted a deep, long kiss.

His lips met hers, but briefly, teasingly. Then they slipped away, leaving her hungry for more; slipped away to drop kisses on her forehead, her nose, her closed eyelids. As she tried to reach his lips, he ran the tip of his tongue around her earlobe.

Her breath was coming in great gasps and her hands moved frantically on his back. It had been so long and her need was so great. But she knew Mark. She knew that the pressure of his body on hers did not mean a quick culmination of their passion. He liked to stretch it out, to make it last a long long time, to drive her almost to distraction with longing, so that their final joining would be one long, continuous ecstasy for her.

And he knew exactly how to do it, she thought, as he slid downward once more, hands and mouth moving hungrily. She twisted in the bed. She moaned. She even considered imploring him to assuage this longing that had become almost a physical pain to her. But she did not. He was recreating that first time together. And his memory of it was surprisingly accurate.

When finally he threw himself down beside her, she knew what he expected. It was her turn. Her turn to explore the fascinating male body that lay so obligingly before her. Just as she had then, and breathing just as heavily, she pushed herself to her knees. Her hands roamed his body then, and in spite of the intervening years, it seemed much the same, the well-cared-for body of a strong, athletic man.

Her exploring fingers traced a curve of scar tissue

under the hair that covered his ribs, and her heart jumped. He'd been wounded. But she made no comment, just kept on with her exploration, lips following where fingers had been. The taste and feel of his body was so familiar. She seemed to know every bit of it and she gloried in that knowledge.

As she knelt there beside him, the years between fell away. She felt again the terrifying yet wonderful passion of her youth. And she gave herself up to it, forgetting everything but her clamoring need.

Then he was sitting up, pushing her down on her back, his body covering hers. "Yes," she whispered. "Oh yes."

She opened herself to him. As eagerly as that young and innocent Claudia had, she opened herself to him, glorying in the feel of his strong thighs against hers, in the pressure of his body as he moved against her willing flesh.

"Oh, Mark!" She could not help crying out as their union became complete, could not help clutching spasmodically at his shoulders, arching her eager body to meet his.

And then that tightly wound spring inside her began to uncoil. It was not a sudden, swift explosion, but a slow, sweet unwinding, so that ecstasy seemed to spread from her center outward in slow ripples of joy.

His labored breath beat against her ear, his seeking mouth covered hers, and the slow, sweet unwinding suddenly became an overwhelming joy that hit all the cells in her body in one swift, breathtaking second. And she cried out with the joy of it, cried out and hugged him to her as his breathing turned to a hoarse gasp and he collapsed against her.

She was soaring. She was so marvelously happy, so

content, that nothing could ever hurt her again. She lay utterly relaxed beneath him, satisfaction infusing her very core.

She tried to hang on to the feeling, so ephemeral that already it was slipping away from her, so fleeting that already she could not quite remember the absolute joy of it. She sighed, and he rolled to one side, drawing her close against him.

"Thank you, Claudia," he whispered against her hair. "Thank you for bringing me back to life."

9

~~~~~~~~~~~~~~

The next morning Claudia woke late. For a moment she wondered at her utter sense of contentment. She felt completely relaxed and satisfied. Then memories of the night before came flooding back.

She had stayed in Mark's room quite late. Lying in each other's arms, they had talked and laughed about the old neighborhood, old friends, old times. It had been very good.

There were some things she hadn't told him, of course. That their weekend together had been her first with a man. That she had waited and waited for the letters that never came. That she had cried herself to sleep on innumerable nights.

She sighed and stretched. All of that was really not Mark's fault. She could see that clearly enough now. For him it had been an interlude—a good one, since he had remembered it for so long—but just an interlude, nevertheless.

If she had not been so young, so naive, so madly in love with her image of him, she could have seen that for herself. And been spared a lot of misery.

She rolled onto her side and looked at her bedside clock. What should she do with this free day? She could go back to the School of Dance. She shook her head; she didn't want to see that beautiful young woman again. Or hear her call Mark by his first name.

She watched a speck of dust caught in a golden beam of sunlight float gently downward. She could go out and explore this new city. There were temples and houses, bazaars and shops, fascinating things and people just waiting to be discovered.

But she didn't want to go alone. It was no fun to see new things if there was no one to share them with. Her eyes strayed to the phone and, alone in the bed, she flushed guiltily. She really wanted to be with Mark. This city—and all the rest of them—meant little to her without him.

Oh, she had a scholar's curiosity; she would never lose that. But what she had with Mark was something more, something different. There was no way a city, no matter how strange and exotic it might be, could generate the kind of excitement, the feeling of being completely alive that she felt when Mark looked at her, when he touched her.

No other man had ever been able to do that to her . . . for her. She closed her eyes against the sudden welling of tears. Probably no man would ever be able to do it again. She tried not to think of that. She must think only of the trip, of this brief interlude that they would have together.

She was not sure, of course, that Mark would even call her again. She could not be sure of anything about him, not after that first experience. But this time she was determined to be prepared. This time she would expect nothing, nothing more than what she already had.

Yes, that was the way to think about it. Last night was hers. It always would be. No one could ever take it away. She would be content with that. She threw back the covers and stretched again, a satisfied smile on her lips. If Mark felt half as good as she did . . .

She was out of the shower, eyeing her two pants suits and wishing she had brought more clothes, when the sharp shrilling of the phone made her jump. It was Mark! It had to be Mark!

She forced herself to take several deep breaths before she picked it up. "Hello."

"Good morning, Claudia."

Her knees went suddenly weak and she sank down on the edge of the bed. "Good morning, Mark."

"I hope I didn't wake you."

"No, no, I've been up for a while."

"I thought you'd sleep late. That's why I didn't call earlier. Listen, I'm downstairs." He laughed softly, sheepishly. "I wanted to let you sleep, but I was afraid of missing you. Can we have breakfast? I'd like to show you around the town. Would you like that?"

The hand that held the receiver trembled. "Yes, Mark." At least her voice was calm. "I'm just dressing. I'll be down soon."

"Take your time," he said, and his voice was a caress. "We have all day."

She stared at the phone for a full minute after she replaced the receiver. She could hardly believe it. Another day, a whole day, with Mark.

Suddenly galvanized into action, she spun toward the closet. What to wear? Oh, if only she had something new, something nice. But she didn't. She settled, finally, on her pale blue dress and sandals. At least it would be cool.

As she stood before the mirror, brushing her hair, she eyed herself critically. There was no denying it. In some indefinable way her body had changed. It looked younger, prettier, and . . . She hesitated over the thought, but it was true. Her body looked sexier. Now, if only Mark saw it that way.

As she stepped off the elevator, he rose from his chair and came swiftly toward her. His cream-colored suit and shirt set off his handsome darkness, and the look of welcome in his eyes sent shivers of desire over her.

She cast a quick glance around the lobby, wondering if any of the others were around. But she and Mark were the only Americans in sight.

"Claudia." He took both her hands in his and for a moment she thought he would lean over and kiss her. But he only asked, "Did you sleep well?"

His eyes were full of laughter and she smiled dryly. "Yes, very well."

He tugged impatiently at her hands. "Let's get out of here. I've so much to show you."

As she followed him across the lobby, she was aware of two distinct and paradoxical feelings. She was glad that no one from the class saw them. She did not want to have to make explanations, especially to

Dell. But she was also disappointed. There was a part of her that would have liked to have the whole world know, to shout from the housetops that Mark wanted her, needed her, loved—

Her thoughts stopped there and recoiled. No, she mustn't think such things. Wanted and needed, they were okay. But loved, no. Mark did not love her. He never had. That was one lesson she had learned in the most difficult way, one lesson she could not afford to forget.

The heat of the city beat at her briefly as they stepped from the air-conditioned lobby. Mark smiled. "You'll get used to it."

She was not at all sure of that. Northern Ohio, even in the summer, was a far cry from this.

"Thailand has a monsoon tropical climate," Mark said as they joined the throngs in the street. "It's more comfortable during the cool season, November to January." He tucked her arm in his. "But that would have interfered with regular classes. And, of course, it's even hotter in the hot season, February to May. This is the rainy season."

Claudia glanced at the sky. "It's so blue and beautiful. Surely it can't rain today."

He laughed and squeezed her arm. "We'll just have to wait and see. Now what do you know about Thailand?"

"Very little, I'm afraid." She looked at the crowd filling Bangkok's streets. "Except what I saw yesterday and"—she laughed—"leftover impressions from *The King and I*."

He laughed too. "Well then, I'll just give you a grand tour of the city. Let's see now." His eyes narrowed thoughtfully. "I think we'll start with a temple. The national religion is Buddhism."

He nodded toward a saffron-robed monk standing patiently, and silently, by the sidewalk. "Every young man spends at least three months as a monk. Many do their stint during the Buddhist equivalent of Lent—the rainy season here."

"Is he begging?" Claudia asked, seeing the bowl in the man's hands.

"Not exactly. He can't ask for money. Or earn it. But other people may gain merit by their generosity in giving to him."

"Sort of like Christian charity," Claudia observed.

Mark grinned. "I guess that depends on your denomination. This kind of charity is widely practiced in Buddhist countries. At least, direct one-to-one giving is. These people haven't institutionalized their giving. They don't keep their poor hidden away."

Claudia nodded. "Is the whole nation Buddhist?"

Mark shook his head. "No. Anyone is free to preach and practice any other faith. There are a few Thai Moslems, Confucians, and Christians.

"There." Mark pointed to a large building looming up in the distance. "There's Wat Phra Keo."

Claudia stopped. The building was very large, its overlapping roofs of slanted tile giving it the look the world recognized as oriental. "Does *wat* mean temple?" she asked as they moved on toward it.

"Yes. Actually it refers to the entire compound. The monks live there. The main shrine hall—the *bot*—faces east. Women are not allowed inside."

"Why not?"

"Ah . . ." He looked slightly uncomfortable. "Bud-

117

dhists don't regard women as equals, at least religious-ly." He hurried on.

"Why aren't the women here doing something about being considered second-class citizens?" she asked.

"They are."

She was relieved to find that he was treating her question with the seriousness it deserved.

"Christianity hasn't exactly had the best record where women are concerned."

"I know."

"Women here are moving into positions of leader-ship, particularly in big business and real estate man-agement. The management of land is probably easier for them to break into because traditionally a Thai father left his cash to his sons, and his land and cattle to his daughters. So you see, they weren't really that bad off."

She considered replying to this, but had to concede that he was right.

His hand slid down from her elbow to take her hand. "The next order of business is to take a ride in a *klong*."

Claudia remembered the guidebook pictures of the canals that crisscrossed the city and the boats that plied the waterways. They reminded her of Venice. It would be fun to ride on one. And romantic.

As Mark helped her into the gondola-like boat with its curious dragon-carved prow, she couldn't help smiling. The day was just beautiful. Everything seemed perfect. The weather, the city, and, most of all, being with Mark.

The nagging little thought that popped into her

mind, that such perfection couldn't possibly last, she pushed immediately away. She would stick to her resolution; she would enjoy what she had and not always be longing for what she didn't have.

Settling into the seat, she found Mark's arm around her shoulders. "Relax," he said. "Enjoy the ride."

She did that, leaning back against him, relishing the feel of his body. She was tempted to close her eyes, so relaxed did she feel. But she kept them open, attending to the various sights he pointed out.

It was like some lovely dream, watching a fairy-tale city move by, and she wished it would last forever. But eventually they reached their destination and Mark helped her out again.

"I want to show you Timland," he said. "It's a kind of Thailand in miniature. I'd like to show you the Ancient City, too. It's got scale models of lost ruins." He frowned. "But it's outside the city. Too far to go today. Maybe next time."

His eyes lingered on her face as he said this, and she fought to keep her features composed as she calmly replied, "Maybe," not letting her eyes meet his.

Then they were back in the bustle of the crowded streets. Everyone seemed to be going somewhere—and enjoying it, Claudia mused as she recognized, or thought she recognized, several groups of tourists. Though the population of the city was extremely cosmopolitan, it was easy to spot these tourists by their ever-present cameras.

"Are you getting hungry?" Mark asked. "I bet you didn't have any breakfast. And it's past lunchtime."

Claudia laughed. "I didn't and I am. But I never realized it until you asked. Do you know a good restaurant around here?" She laughed again. "Of course you do. That's why you asked me if I'm hungry, right?"

"Right."

He squeezed her hand. It felt natural to go hand in hand with him now. "What kind of food do you feel like?" he asked. "We can get Chinese. And there are many places serving good American food."

"I'd like to try some more Thai food," she replied, and, catching the flicker of joy in his eyes, wondered why that should please him so.

"Good. I know just the place."

"But not too spicy," she hastened to add.

"The chopped red chillies are the worst," he said, grinning. "But we'll be careful. What did you eat last night?"

"Chicken and mushroom stew. I can't remember its Thai name. It was spicy, but not hot spicy."

He nodded. "We can have fried tender beef with ginger, or sweet and sour pork, or sweet and sour fish."

"Sweet and sour fish?" she interrupted him. "That sounds different. And good."

"Then that's what we'll have."

And they did, along with some other Thai dishes Mark wanted her to experience. Then they returned to their tour of the city. By the time they turned back toward the hotel, Claudia's head was swimming. "If only I can remember half of what you've told me," she said.

"I'm glad you enjoyed the day," he replied, his eyes growing serious. "Claudia, have dinner with me and . . . and come back up to my room. Please."

She forced herself to hesitate, to appear to be

considering, but she knew she would not refuse. She didn't intend to let go of this perfect day until she had to. They might only have this brief interlude, but she was going to make the most of it.

"Yes," she said, lifting her eyes to his. "I'll do that. I'd like to do that."

10

～～～～～～～～

As the door to Mark's room closed behind her, Claudia felt a growing sense of embarrassment. The thought had occurred to her during dinner, a lovely dinner in a tiny Thai restaurant, and had haunted her ever since. She should have returned to her room to shower and change before dinner. And, most especially, before their lovemaking. They had been on the streets all day. She was not tired, but she felt dusty and dirty, especially now that Mark would be kissing and caressing her.

He turned from locking the door and drew her into his arms. "Oh, Claudia. I've been wanting to do this all day." And he kissed her thoroughly.

She kissed him back, of course, but her concern got in the way and she could not completely let go. He released her and looked down at her with a frown. "Is something wrong?"

She managed a little laugh, but it caught in her throat. "I . . . I need a shower."

He laughed too, and hugged her to him so tightly she squealed for breath. He grinned as he released her. "Is that all?"

She laughed more fully then, her embarrassment vanishing. "Yes."

He kissed the tip of her nose. "That's easily taken care of, you know. I could use a shower myself."

"Do you want to go first," she asked, "or shall I?"

He grinned, looking younger by the minute. "Neither."

"I don't understand."

"We go together," he said, reaching behind her for the zipper on her dress.

"Together?"

He pulled the zipper down. "That's right. Together." His eyes danced. "They say it's great fun."

She stared at him. Together. In the shower. It was not an idea that would have occurred to her. And yet . . .

"After all," he said, his mouth moving down her bare shoulder as her dress slid to the floor, "it's not like you have parts I haven't seen."

That was true, she admitted as his hands reached for the back of her bra. Mark had explored every inch of her body as she had his. It had seemed perfectly right at the time. And now it seemed right that they should shower together.

She slid her feet out of her sandals and shed her half-slip and panties. "I think I have some bobby pins in my purse. Let me pin up my hair."

He touched her breast in a swift caress. "Don't take too long, sweet."

She smiled at the endearment and, capturing his hand, put a moist kiss in his palm.

His eyes danced. "Hurry up or I'll beat you into the shower." And his hands flew to his shirt buttons.

She hurried to her purse and dug into its depths where she found half a dozen loose bobby pins. But when she turned to the mirror, she found that her hands were unsteady.

"Hurry," came Mark's voice from the bathroom.

"I am hurrying," she called back, pinning her gathered hair haphazardly on top of her head.

She could hear the sound of running water as she hurried toward the bathroom. She paused in the doorway. "Here I am."

Mark stood beside the tub and she caught her breath at the sight of his body. She was not the sort to stare at men or to evaluate their looks, but to her eyes Mark seemed perfect. He was just the right height. He took care of himself. His stomach was hard and flat, his chest well muscled. She smiled, wondering how his chest hair would feel wet, or the finer hair on his legs.

"Has anyone ever told you you have great legs?" she asked. She was a little surprised at herself, at her feeling of fun. But she supposed there was no reason why lovemaking must always be serious. There had been a lot of fun and laughter that first weekend. She would never forget that. Or this trip, she thought, then hurriedly pushed the thought from her mind. Here and now. She was going to concentrate on the here and now.

He turned back to the shower to check the water, but she caught his grin. "Oh, of course I get compliments on my great legs. Every single day."

"Don't be silly," she said. "I'm serious." But she was grinning, too. "You have great legs. Of course, your chest's pretty nice, too."

She was beside him now and he turned suddenly and caught her in his arms. "You've got some pretty nice parts yourself," he said, and kissed her forehead. His eyes dropped to her lips, but he shook his head. "First things first, Hanson." He offered her his hand. "If you'll just step into the shower here, we'll see what we can do."

She took his hand, stepping into the tub. He followed her, pulling the shower curtain closed behind him. "And now . . ."

She was prepared for the water, but she was not prepared to find it icy cold. She squealed and jumped —jumped in the only direction possible, right into his arms.

He grinned. "Good thinking, huh?"

She shivered. "It's too cold."

"It's just invigorating," he teased. "But I'll fix it."

He leaned around her to adjust the water and she glanced down at the play of muscles under his gleaming wet skin. Their moment of contact had been brief, but she was intrigued by the feel of his wet body against her own. The sensation was very different. Wet, of course, and almost slippery. And very very exciting.

He straightened and put his arms around her again. "There, that should be better."

"Thank you." She felt a sudden surge of embarrassment as she looked up into his eyes.

"Well," he said, "shall I do the honors first?"

"What honors?"

"Why, washing you."

She flushed. She couldn't help it. "You're going to wash me?"

"Exactly. And then you can wash me. Won't that be fun?"

"I'm not exactly sure," she replied, but she answered his smile with one of her own. Since she was going to do this rather crazy thing, she might as well enjoy it.

As she watched, he took a cloth and soaped it thoroughly. "Now stand still," he said with a smile, "and I won't get soap in your eyes."

He didn't, either. It gave her the most curious feeling to have him washing her face. There was nothing at all erotic about it. But there was such tenderness to it that she had to swallow a sudden lump in her throat and blink back the tears.

He rinsed her face and throat, then soaped the cloth again. "Front or back first?" he asked.

She shook her head. "It doesn't matter. You're the expert."

The glance he gave her was an odd one, and she wondered what sore spot she had inadvertently touched.

"I don't think what we're doing now falls into the category of drama," he replied. "That's the one thing I can claim to be expert in. And even *that* claim I don't make." His hand moved down the slope of her shoulder to where her breast quivered expectantly.

"Such modesty." She tried to keep her voice even as his soapy hands encircled one breast, but she couldn't refrain from murmuring, "Mmmm. That feels good."

He soaped the front of her liberally—that breast,

then the other, then down across her rib cage to the slight roundness of her belly, and down to her legs, quivering slightly now from the intensity of the feelings his hands were raising in her. She braced herself with her hands on his shoulders as he bent to his task.

When he straightened, she let her hands slide down his arms. "Hold me," she begged. "I want to feel you against me."

He grinned. "Anything to oblige a lady." And he took her in his arms.

The soap made the sensations she was feeling different. Now they were definitely slippery. She giggled like a young girl. "I wish we had one of those things—'slip and slide,' they called them. We had one when I was little."

He chuckled. "I remember. I had one, too. It was plastic and you ran water down it from the garden hose and then slid on it."

"Right. Only I'd like one to lie on—all soapy like this."

His grin widened. "I get the picture. Only with something kind of soft underneath it."

"Yes." She moved slightly, delighting in the feel of their soapy bodies. "That would be fun."

He agreed. "But I'm afraid it would make for rather uncomfortable sleeping afterward."

She giggled again as her mind presented her with a picture of a bed awash in soapsuds and only Mark's head visible. "Yes, I guess it would."

His hands moved across her back. "Well, it's too bad, but we'll just have to make do with a bed." His eyes grew speculative, and he glanced at the bathroom floor. "Of course, if we had enough towels . . ."

She laughed and hugged him. "The bed will be

fine," she insisted. "But you haven't washed my back yet."

He was holding her close against him, their warm soapy bodies as near as they could get. His face was close to hers, so close. Without thinking, she raised herself, sliding her slippery body upward until her lips reached his.

His arms tightened around her as he returned the kiss. By the time he had finished and drawn his mouth slightly back from hers, she was aflame with desire. Against her breasts she felt the wet wiry hair of his chest. His thighs were close against hers, and his hard maleness . . .

She sighed and clung to him, her legs quivering with desire. "I don't know how much longer I can stand up," she whispered.

He held her off a little. "There'll be no rush jobs when I'm in charge of operations." His eyes danced. "Besides, it's your own fault. You shouldn't have kissed me like that."

She smiled. "Then you shouldn't have held me like that."

He frowned, but his eyes still danced. "Shall we have an academic-style debate here, or should we get on with what we were doing?"

"Oh, by all means, let's get on with what we were doing."

He grinned again. "That's good. 'Cause I'm getting anxious for my turn. Let me see your back."

She turned slowly. The narrow confines of the tub-shower made it easy for her to brush her body against his accidentally as she moved. She smiled as he began to wash her shoulders, down her back to her waist and beyond.

"Easy now," he commanded as the soapy cloth approached her most secret place. She felt a wave of desire so strong she had to clench her fists to keep from throwing herself into his arms again.

Then he was straightening, his hands on her upper arms turning her back to face him. "Now for a good rinse." And he backed her slowly under the shower.

The warm water cascading down her aroused body was incredibly sensuous. She closed her eyes, every sense heightened.

His lips touched hers. One brief contact, then they were gone. Her eyes flew open.

"Your turn," he said, offering her the cloth.

She took it with a hand that trembled slightly, not from fear, but from desire, and soaped it good. Then she reached up to wash his face. The dark stubble of his beard was coarse against her fingertips. He had not shaved since morning, of course.

With his eyes closed against the soap, he seemed younger, more vulnerable. She had a sudden picture of him as a little boy of six or seven, squirming with impatience while his mother washed his face. She could not remember him at that age, of course. She had not yet been born. But she could imagine.

She washed his neck and ears, then rinsed them carefully. "You can open your eyes now," she told him.

"Good. I like to watch you."

Ignoring the urge to lean against him, she soaped up his chest, swirling the soapy hair into patterns, pulling it into soapy peaks.

Glancing down, he grinned. "I'm beginning to feel like a walking finger painting."

She laughed. "That's so appropriate. I was just

remembering how we used to finger-paint in school. The smoothness of the paint and the paper. This texture is different." She wrinkled her nose at him. "But nice."

"Maybe we should start a new industry," he said. "Soap paints."

She shook her head. "Too late. I think it's already been done. For kids. I've seen the ads somewhere."

He shrugged soapy shoulders. "Oh, well, it was a good idea."

Her hands had moved to his flat belly, and as they began their downward progress he closed his eyes. There was silence in the room for several minutes, nothing but the sound of the air-conditioner and his increasingly labored breathing.

"Enough," he said suddenly. "Better move on, or you won't get the chance to do the rest of me."

Obediently she moved on, down his legs, noting the difference in texture of the fine wet hair there. "Turn around," she said.

She worked upward from his feet then, soaping his hard behind and his strong back. Then she moved him under the spray. "All done."

The soap was barely rinsed away before he had his arms around her again. "Now we're both squeaky clean," he whispered, his tongue at her ear.

"Yes." She kissed his neck.

"Good. Then what do you say we get out of here and dry off?" His eyes danced. "I'd like to swoop you up in my arms and carry you to the bed like that, all glistening wet. But, since I have to sleep in it later . . ."

He drew back the shower curtain and stepped out, offering her his hand. As she joined him on the bath mat, he handed her a towel and took one himself. "Beat you to the bed."

He already had himself half-dried before she realized what he was saying, but she was right behind him as he headed for the bed and pulled down the covers.

For a moment they stood in silence on opposite sides of the bed. Then he laughed and threw himself down and she followed him, their bodies rolling automatically toward the middle, toward each other.

He sighed as they made contact, and lightly kissed her nose. "You feel so good."

Wriggling even closer against him, she kissed his forehead. "You, too."

For a moment they lay without moving, content in the feel of each other. Then his mouth moved to cover hers.

She had thought she was aroused. With all that foreplay in the shower she could hardly be otherwise. But this kiss fanned the flames even higher. She could feel the stubble of his beard against her chin as his mouth devoured hers. She pressed against him, her body molding itself against his, her hands clutching his shoulders.

He kissed her long and hard; and her body, so long wanting, clamored for the joining with his. When he released her lips, she gasped against his. "Please, Mark. Please."

"Yes." His voice was deep, hoarse, and he rolled to his knees to kneel over her. His eyes slid along her eager body like another caress. Then he was lowering himself on her and she opened for him, eagerly, happily, a long sigh of joy bubbling out of her throat at their joining.

For several minutes he lay quiet, but her body would not be denied and she moved against him, vaguely aware that this was different and that she liked it.

Suddenly he took up the rhythm, moving first slowly, then faster and faster. And all the feelings, all the ecstasy that had been gathering in her body since they had come into this room seemed sucked into the center of her being. There, like a giant whirlpool, they spun faster and faster, grew larger and larger until, as he collapsed against her with a hoarse exclamation, this pool of joy sped outward, sending waves of warmth to inundate her whole trembling body.

This was joy—the epitome of joy. Two halves made whole, said some foggy part of her mind. For surely this ecstasy, this ultimate joy, was one of completeness, born out of the innate knowledge that this was how it could be, how it should be between men and women. However brief the moment, it was a moment of satisfaction, of completion so perfect that she could imagine nothing better.

For long moments they lay silent, content with the feel of each other's body. If only they could remain like this, Claudia thought. She felt so peaceful, so content. He rolled over, pulling her against him, and she lay there, perfectly relaxed.

Slowly, however, she came back to reality. She should get up; she should go back to her own hotel, her own room. But she felt too peaceful to move. How nice it would be, her mind suggested gently, to lie here till morning, to wake up with Mark beside her, his arm around her as it was now. How pleasant to wake up that way every morning.

She was halfway into the fantasy before she realized

what she was doing. Awareness hit her almost like a blow and she had to force herself to lie still, to breathe slowly and calmly, to remember that she was concerned only with the here and now. Thoughts of the future had no place in this relationship. It was temporary, very temporary.

When she felt that she had herself under control, she stirred against him. "Mark, I have to go back to my hotel tonight."

He sighed. "Yes, I know. And we have an early flight, so we can't sleep late." His arms contracted, holding her tightly against him. "I don't like to let you go."

She didn't reply to that. There were too many emotions too close to the surface for her to try to talk.

He kissed her once more, a brief kiss this time, then swung himself up to a sitting position. "I'll take you back now."

11

~oooooooooo~

Late the next afternoon, with Dell beside her, Claudia took a seat in a classroom at the University of Rangoon. She was tired from the flight to Burma; this jumping around on airplanes was not an everyday thing to her. And to add to that, she had not slept well. Although Mark had returned her to her room fairly early, sleep had escaped her until almost dawn. Dell's insistence on sitting by her on the plane had eliminated any chance of resting there, and the brief nap she had snatched after their arrival hadn't helped much.

She took a deep breath and tried to clear her head. She and Mark had not been alone together yet that day, had not spoken more than the conventional words of greeting. She recognized that such a course was sensible; she certainly didn't want to be the object of gossip. But some part of her was upset by it and kept insisting that after the last two nights, after all that had happened between them, this polite formality was wrong.

As Mark entered, deep in conversation with several students, she forced herself to remain calm. Reaching the front of the room, he glanced out over the assembled class. He was smiling, of course. He always did when he spoke to them. But it was the friendly, impersonal smile that he gave everyone. Even though she knew it was foolish, she longed for that special, tender smile he had worn last night.

Then she gave herself a mental shake and settled down to listen. She didn't want her passion for Mark to interfere with assimilating this new material. Woman though she might be—as her hours with Mark had proven so delightfully—she was first and foremost a scholar. And this drama was one of the most intriguing things she had studied for a long time.

"Now," Mark said. "Just a few words before we go to the auditorium. We'll be seeing a piece of a Rama play, Burmese style. Notice how this more popular form differs from the classical Thai form. Burmese dance-drama is descended from the Thai but has absorbed more popular elements."

A hand went up. "Yes?" Mark said.

"I thought the Rama plays were given at night here."

Claudia looked at the speaker—one of those girls who hung around Mark. She felt a sharp twinge of jealousy.

"That's true," Mark said. "It happens that a class here at the university is in rehearsal for a performance to be given in several weeks. They're going to do a piece of it for us."

He smiled at the class. "Traditionally the Rama play

is done at night. It used to take up to twenty-one nights. Now it takes only ten to twelve. Performances generally last all night. Other dances are done first, before the play starts at midnight."

He glanced at his watch. "Time to move to the auditorium."

As they entered the auditorium, Claudia wished she could be closer to Mark. If only she could sit beside him; if only they were alone here. The play would be much more fun if she could share it with him. She suppressed a sigh. That wasn't possible, of course.

The auditorium seemed huge with only their small group in it. As the students arranged themselves on the mats, Claudia glanced around. She had tried to place herself more or less on the edge of the group, hoping that Mark might accidentally sit beside her. But as the music began and the lights dimmed, she saw he was still standing.

"Notice the demon masks," Mark told the group.

Claudia's eyes were caught by the costumes, interwoven with shimmering threads of gold and silver. The dancers moved with pure grace. A smooth supple flow of hand, foot, arm, leg. Every movement a miniature work of art.

"This part," continued Mark, "is from Book Four. Rama has helped the monkey, Sugriva, wrest control of the monkey kingdom from his evil brother, Bali. Sugriva and his monkey army help Rama fight the wicked Ravana, who has kidnapped Rama's wife."

As the music crescendoed, a fierce battle ensued on the stage. Warriors and monkeys, both masked, fought ferociously, their acrobatic feats almost incredible to behold. Claudia watched eagerly, drinking in every detail.

As a dramatic form, she thought, Asian theater had many advantages. This battle was exciting partly because the music built audience emotions to a high pitch. Something else pushed at her consciousness. Some other music used to heighten dramatic moments. Used specifically for that purpose. Of course! In the old silent movies! She smiled to herself, remembering some she had seen on tape with their melodramatic piano accompaniments.

And then another realization hit her. There was one form of American drama—the most popular, too—in which music played a big role, though until this very moment she had not really thought about it. Movie sound tracks all had musical backgrounds. Generally, the music was less dramatic than in the old days, but sometimes— And it was used to create the proper mood.

She wondered if Mark had considered this angle. He probably had. But he hadn't mentioned it to the class. Without thinking, she turned to look for him and met the direct gaze of his eyes.

Everyone else was looking at the stage. And that was a good thing, she thought, as the warmth swept through her. For the way he was looking at her now . . . Certain things they had done the night before rushed into her thoughts. The touch of his hands, of his lips, the feel of his body against her own. For a long moment their eyes held and she saw in his the look of recognition and warmth that she had been craving.

A loud clash of cymbals almost made her jump, and she turned hastily back toward the stage, now liberally strewn with fallen warriors.

Beside her Dell stirred and whispered something

about "racket." She didn't try to reply to him. If Dell wanted to dislike everything he wasn't familiar with, that was his business.

When the performance was over, Mark announced, "That's all the scheduled events for today. You'll find other possibilities listed in your handouts. The professors here have asked me to tell you they will be glad to talk to anyone who has questions. If you are interested in the great Burmese actor U Po Sein, there is someone in the next room to give you information."

Claudia got to her feet with the others. U Po Sein. She remembered the name from her reading. But they were covering so much territory and she had read so much, it was hard to remember everything.

She looked for Mark as she made her way to the door, but he was again surrounded by students. She sighed.

Beside her, Dell grinned. "Well, that's more than enough for me," he declared. "Shall we go see the sights? This place must have some night spots. But first I think I'll sample some of the native brew."

Claudia shook her head. "No thanks. I want to look around here."

Dell frowned. "You take this whole thing too seriously, girl. Lighten up. Live a little."

She tried to control her irritation. Dell couldn't know how it annoyed her to be called "girl." He had no social consciousness at all. And very little scholarly sense, either, she supposed. She managed a small smile as she replied dryly, "I *am* living. This is my idea of fun."

Dell shook his head. "Well, it's sure not mine. See you around."

With a sigh of relief Claudia turned toward the room where the professor waited. A small Burman in a Western suit sat at a table grading papers. He looked up as she paused in the door and smiled. "Hello. Come in, please. Can I help you?" he asked with the British accent she had heard so often lately.

"My name is Claudia Carstairs. Mark . . . Dr. Hanson said there would be someone here to tell us about U Po Sein."

The Burman nodded. "That is me. Professor San Thaik. If you will sit down"—he indicated a chair—"I will answer your questions."

Claudia's laugh revealed her embarrassment. "I'm afraid I don't know enough to ask any questions. All I know is that U Po Sein was a great actor."

She took the chair he had indicated. "I am a student of Shakespeare," she explained. "And, more specifically, of a great English actor, Edmund Kean."

"Oh, yes. During the English Regency," Professor San replied.

She must have let her surprise show, for he smiled gently. "With the English theater I have some familiarity. A great actor, Kean. Very great."

"Tell me about U Po Sein," she said.

The professor nodded. "He was a performer in the *zat pwe*—our classical dance play—which is devoted to Burmese history. It was he who first conceived of doing the Jataka stories, which had previously only been done in our *yokthe pwe,* a puppet show."

Claudia smiled. Here was an example of the puppet theater preceding the live actors! Perhaps she was right in her feeling that it had come first.

"This he did shortly before World War I," the

Burman continued. "A very great man, U Po Sein. In 1919 the British government honored him with a medal for his service to the crown."

"The first actor in all of Southeast Asia to be so honored by a government," said a familiar voice, and Mark crossed the room to take a seat beside her.

"Mark. How are you?"

"Fine, Thaik. And you?"

Their exchange of greetings gave Claudia time to gather her wits. She glanced quickly toward the door but no one seemed to have followed him. She brought her attention back to the men near her.

"Mark here can tell you all about Po Sein," Professor San was saying. "He is an expert on the man."

Mark shrugged. "Now, Thaik, I got a great deal of my information from you, my friend."

The Burman nodded. "Yes, that is true." He leaned forward, his formality falling away. "Listen, Mark, you are in luck. There's a *zat pwe* tonight. I'll give you the address." He smiled at Claudia. "Perhaps you'd like to take your friend."

She fought the rising wave of color. How did this man know about them?

Mark didn't seem at all perturbed. "Yes, I think that would be fun." He turned and gave her the kind of smile she'd been yearning for. "Don't you, Claudia?"

She nodded. "Yes. Yes, I do."

As the two men continued their discussion, she tried to listen, to absorb everything they were saying. But the fascinating life of Po Sein, who in the Burmese custom had had more than one wife, kept being shoved aside by the strength of her feelings for Mark. He had let Professor San—no, he had encouraged Professor San—to think of them as a couple. She was aware that she very much liked the idea; was aware, too, that she shouldn't. She must not let herself begin to think that way, to feel possessive. That could be—would be—very dangerous.

Some time later Professor San looked at his watch. "I am sorry, Mark," he said, reverting to his formal manner again. "But I must leave now. I have a class to meet."

"Of course." Mark glanced at his own watch. "I didn't realize we'd been here so long."

The Burman turned to Claudia. "I hope you enjoy your trip, Miss Carsfairs." His eyes sparkled. "And your visit to the *zat pwe*. Perhaps I will see you there."

He wrote swiftly. "Here is the address, Mark. You can find it easily, I'm sure."

"Thanks, Thaik." Mark got to his feet and Claudia followed. "See you later."

As they made their way out the door and down the hall, Mark turned to her. "I hoped you'd go to see Thaik. I knew you'd like him."

"You seem to know someone everywhere we stop," she said.

He nodded. "Of course. I've spent years traveling this route. Listen, do you have plans for the rest of the day?"

"I . . . No." The word was out before she could stop it.

"Good. Then I can show you Rangoon." He stopped right outside the door and looked at her as the people on the sidewalk flowed around them. "That is, if you'll let me."

It took her by surprise, this way he had of almost pleading with her. It was so unlike the old days, so unlike the time when he had taken it for granted that

141

she was ready to go anywhere with him. What had changed him? she wondered. Was it the tragedy of losing his family that had robbed him of that joyous certainty? Or was it just age, the natural result of the process of living?

She didn't know and she couldn't ask. She liked his concern for her, his desire to respect her wishes, but sometimes she wished for that old Mark, the one who had been so confident he knew everything.

"Of course I'll let you." She laughed. "Where else could I get such a reliable guide? And for free, yet."

Late that evening, or rather, early the next morning, she and Mark left the *zat pwe*. It no longer seemed so strange to be surrounded by people seated on mats. And surrounded they had been. The audience held people of all ages. Two mats away from them a baby had slept peacefully. On another, two lovers sat hand in hand. Here sat a whole family, the children engrossed in their toys or nibbling on fruit. There two young women conversed.

The noise level had seemed very high to one used to Western standards. She thought of this as they turned toward the hotel. "It doesn't seem like a theater," she said. "No one is quiet."

He smiled. "I guess it's more like one of our ball games. Or maybe an outdoor concert."

"How can anyone understand what's going on?"

Mark squeezed her hand. "You're forgetting, the audience knows these stories. Like you know 'Snow White.' Or 'Cinderella.' Or one of Shakespeare's plays." He smiled, pleased to have found a comparison he liked.

"But I couldn't hear."

"What they say isn't so important. There's the movement."

"You mean the dance part."

"Yes. And the gestures."

"I can see why you wanted to study this drama. It's so different."

He nodded, slowing his pace so that they moved smoothly with the crowd around them. "Yes, I like the differences. But I like the similarities, too. You know, finding universals."

"Yes." She recalled her earlier insight and hurried to share it with him. "Remember when you were talking about musical motifs? How they indicate theme and character?"

He nodded.

"Well, I was thinking about it and I realized that we have something similar."

"Go on."

She couldn't know that her eyes were sparkling, but she knew there was eagerness in her voice. "The silent movies had their piano accompaniments. And contemporary ones have their background music. It works in much the same way."

"That's right," he said. "You love the theater, don't you, Claudia?"

"Oh yes." She smiled at him. "And now more than ever. I really am glad I came on this trip. I've enjoyed it so much."

In the light of the streetlamps his face looked younger. He dropped her hand and slid his arm around her waist. "So have I, Claudia. So have I."

They were nearing the hotel now and she felt the desire that had been building between them all day. She wanted him. She wanted him badly. Their lovemaking the last two nights only made her want him more.

But always there was reality staring her in the face, harsh reality that kept reminding her of the brevity of their relationship, of the surety of its end.

And besides that there was something else to consider. This time they were not in different hotels. This time all the members of the class had rooms on the same floor, close together. If they were seen going in or coming out of the wrong room . . .

It was going to be difficult enough, once this interlude was over and Mark was gone, to pick up the pieces of her life and go on. She certainly didn't need to have people asking questions or giving her strange looks. Gossiping. And gossip spread easily on a college campus. She knew that.

She tried to pull her mind away, to get back on safe ground. "Which do you think came first?" she asked. "The puppet theater or live actors?"

He considered for a moment. "What do you think?"

"It's hard to say." Ahead, she could see the hotel now. It was difficult to control her thoughts, to keep them on drama. "I was intrigued by Po Sein." They were at the hotel lobby now and she eased herself away from his arm. "By his doing the Jataka stories with live actors, stories that had always been done with puppets before."

Mark listened attentively as she expanded on her theory. He even made some suggestions as they rode up in the elevator with several other guests.

He stopped outside her door, and the smile he gave her threatened to melt her insides. "I love the theater,

Claudia," he said softly. "But that's not what's on my mind now."

The desire blazing in his eyes seemed to set her body on fire. She struggled to retain her common sense. "I can't, Mark. Not here."

He didn't try to argue, didn't try to change her mind. He just smiled a sad smile that seemed to age him ten years. "Good night, Claudia. See you tomorrow."

"Good night, Mark."

He turned and left her then, and she quickly let herself into her room, fighting back the desire to call, to run after him. She was not responsible for Mark Hanson's happiness, she told herself as, with trembling hands, she got ready for bed. She'd do better to start looking out for herself.

She was getting into this too deep. It was one thing to feel sexual attraction for a man. Even to act on it. It was quite another to let herself fall in love again. She had made that mistake once and suffered for it. She didn't intend to do it again.

12

The flight to Jakarta found Dell beside her again. Claudia let his chatter drift in and out of her consciousness. She tried not to think of Mark, but her mind insisted on pointing out to her that the trip was more than half over. She had better think of some way to forget about him. She would have to do so soon anyway.

As always, it was easier to give herself good advice than to follow it. Every time someone moved up or down the aisle her eyes lifted, automatically searching for Mark's face, wishing for one little flicker of tenderness to appear in his eyes as he looked at her.

Though he passed her seat more than once, she did not get her wish. Of course, Dell was right there beside her, as he had been on all their travels. A fact that could hardly have escaped Mark's notice.

She didn't know whether to be pleased or angry at Dell's insistence on hanging around her. She did need a buffer, someone to protect her from Mark's attention in public—attention she was fairly certain she would have been unable to refuse without Dell's presence beside her.

She felt torn. Her time with Mark had been beautiful. Golden hours. But that was just the point. She couldn't expect these golden hours to last. She had convinced herself that she could handle something this brief without being hurt again. But now she was not so sure. In fact, it would probably be better to withdraw from him now, before she stored up any more memories. For, as she knew so well, the more beautiful the memories, the sharper the pain of loss.

This line of thought continued to haunt her through the flight and the trip to the hotel. She could not help an occasional glance in Mark's direction, but she could tell herself that she was glad he didn't try to reach her once she'd gotten to her room. She could tell herself that, but she couldn't quite make herself believe it.

So, when she joined the others in the lobby, she was not in the best of moods.

"More puppets," Dell complained. "And all night long." His face was expressive. "I can think of better things to do with my nights."

She tried to keep from snapping at him, but she was not successful. "I don't suppose it's necessary to see the entire performance."

Dell gave her a strange glance. "Jet lag must be catching up to you."

She didn't bother to answer that, just followed the others into the minivan Mark had hired.

The open-sided pavilion was already crowded, she saw as she descended from the van a little later. Smiling, chattering people reclined or sat on the inevitable mats. Joyous anticipation hung in the air.

"I have some friends reserving space for us." Mark's voice came from so close behind her that she almost jumped. "It's on the puppet side. You can see more there. Later, if you like, you can move to the shadow side."

With Dell grumbling under his breath, they trailed after Mark. By now she should be used to Mark's knowing so many people, she thought as, moving carefully around and over mats, they made their way to their places. Several men awaited them there. Mark greeted them and gestured to the class to sit down. Again she found herself longing to sit beside him. She needed to feel his touch.

Her heart rose up in her throat as he moved toward her. Then he settled himself behind her, near the center of the group, but still close to her. Could he be feeling it too, this terrible need to touch?

"Look at the puppets," he was telling the class around him. "The puppeteer keeps them stuck in that banana log until he needs them. One puppeteer does the whole show. A complete set of puppets consists of three to four hundred."

She heard the sharp intake of someone's breath.

"The performance will begin at eight-thirty, not long now. It'll go on, without any pauses, until the sky turns gray just before dawn. About nine hours."

She couldn't help herself; she had to see his face. She turned toward him. "How can the puppeteer remember so much?" she asked.

His eyes lingered on her face for the briefest of

moments. "He improvises a lot of the dialogue, but the narration and certain standard scenes are set."

"Why are all the puppets in profile?" asked another student.

"Tradition," replied Mark as he turned in that direction. Claudia fought to control her feelings. He was so close. She could just reach out and touch him. To do that seemed the most important thing in the world.

"The characters are easily recognized by the shape of their bodies or heads. Noses in particular show character. You won't be able to understand the words, of course. Songs and narration are done in an archaic dialect. Tonight's story is from the Mahabharata, though Ramayana stories and Javanese animistic ones are also done."

The puppeteer, who had finished sticking the puppets in the banana log while Mark talked, turned toward the little orchestra. Strange, almost shrill tones filled the heavy air. Only now, Claudia heard more than noise. She heard repeating motifs, something more than dissonance.

She shifted her position slightly. It was hard getting used to sitting on mats. Almost harder than learning to see the beauties of this very different music, she thought. Then she froze.

Something was pressing against her. It was Mark's knee; it had to be. Slowly and carefully she finished positioning herself on the mat. But she didn't move away from the pressure of that knee. She heard quite clearly the voice in her head that said she should. But she seemed physically incapable of doing it.

She needed his touch. Maybe he needed hers. But no! She wasn't going to fall into that trap again; she wasn't going to put thoughts in his head or try to figure out what he was thinking. He was touching her. That much was fact. That much she could be sure of. Whether it was by accident or by intent, he was touching her, and that was all she needed to know.

She wrenched her mind back to the stage where the fierce shape of an ogre with his bulging eyes and bulbous nose was carrying on. "Note the faces of certain puppets," Mark was saying. She knew he was speaking to the whole class, but because he was keeping his voice low it had a more intimate sound, almost as though it were meant for her ears alone. "The god Vishnu's face is black—a sign of inner maturity. The one with the white face is of noble descent. The villain over there, on the left of the screen, has a red face that shows his uncontrolled desires and passions."

Uncontrolled desires and passions, Claudia thought. So in this culture, that made one a villain. Funny, she was much more apt to think of those particular emotions as making one a victim.

The puppeteer's voice flowed on, the music behind it accenting every movement. Watching and listening carefully, Claudia observed that the arrival of each character was introduced by a different motif.

Behind her someone asked, "How do they know which character is talking?"

"Everyone knows the story already," Mark explained. "But watch the puppet's arms. They move when the character talks."

And so the play continued, a progression of demons, gods, priests, warriors, and clowns casting their shadows on the screen. They were sharp and intricate shadows, easily recognized by the audience on the other side of the screen.

More than once during the long hours Claudia was forced to change her position. She wondered how people could sit for such long periods without any support for their backs. But every time she shifted, the pressure of Mark's knee remained, warm against her.

She tried to tell herself she was being silly. It was not on purpose that he kept in touch with her body. Wasn't Dell on her left constantly brushing against her? Couldn't she feel the pressure of his leg against hers right at that moment?

But it wasn't the same, replied an insistent voice in her head. It wasn't the same at all. And to prove it she shifted yet again, leaving a little space between them. She held her breath, oblivious to the play, to the theater, to everything around her until she felt again the subtle pressure of Mark's knee.

As the night wore on and it grew later, members of the class rose one by one and drifted away. Beside her, Dell fidgeted and grumbled. Several times he looked directly at her, but she pretended not to notice, to be totally absorbed in the action of the play. Finally it seemed he could stand it no longer. "Claudia."

She had to turn to him then. "Yes?"

"I'm tired."

"Go on back to the hotel," she said, still conscious of the comforting pressure of Mark's knee against her back. "I'll come later."

Dell frowned. "I don't like to leave you here."

"I'll see that Miss Carstairs gets back to the hotel." Mark's voice was extremely formal.

Dell's expression brightened. "Thank you, sir. I

appreciate it." He got to his feet, all his fatigue gone. "See you later."

Claudia nodded. As he made his way across and around the crowded mats, she kept her eyes on the play. She was aware that other people from the class had left, but she didn't know if they had all gone or if those two persistent women students were still near Mark.

And she didn't dare to turn around and look. Not with her heart leaping about in her throat. If someone else should be there, how could she keep her disappointment from showing on her face?

She stared unseeing at the stage, wishing, hoping, almost praying. Then the pressure against her eased and Mark was moving up beside her. "Dell should be out of sight by now," he said.

She felt the length of his warm thigh against her and, unable to help herself, she turned to face him.

There was laughter in his dark eyes. "I thought they'd never all leave. But I was determined to stay to the end, especially if you were."

"It's a very interesting performance," she said primly, but she couldn't keep her eyes from sparkling. "I'm enjoying it immensely."

"Oh, so am I." He shifted a little, moving even closer and putting his arm around her waist. "So am I."

The feel of his body was too much for her, and she let herself lean against him, let herself enjoy the goodness of being close to him.

They sat that way for a long time in great contentment while the drama unfolded on the stage before them. From time to time he explained some point to her, but it was always the soft voice of the lover that he used, not the formal one of the teacher.

The sky was turning gray and dawn was almost there when the puppeteer finished and began to pack away his puppets. The crowd—and it was still a crowd, Claudia saw—got to its feet, stretched, and rolled up the mats. Parents picked up sleeping babies and, rounding up the older children, set out for their homes.

Claudia and Mark rose, too. She stood silently by while he helped to roll up the mats and made his goodbyes. Only then did she think to wonder what his friends had thought. She waited until they were on the street again before she asked him.

"Your friends. They must have thought it odd. I mean . . ."

He shrugged. "All Americans seem strange here. But as for my friends . . . First, they would never say anything about my choice of companions. And second, they would be glad for me. They know it's not good to be alone. In fact, they expect me to marry again eventually."

A sudden lump in her throat prevented her from answering and she blinked back sudden tears. She had been alone for far too long. Perhaps if her mother had not been ill all those years. Or perhaps if she had met another man who affected her as Mark did. But she never had. He was the only one.

They walked silently for some moments, Claudia fighting for control over her emotions. They would soon be back at the hotel, and there they would have to part again. And each parting grew more painful. Awareness of this was growing in her. She tried to regain her resolution, to remind herself that she was only going to think of the here and now. But she was having a hard time of it.

Trying to distract her mind from such painful thoughts, she brought it to focus on the city around them. Though the first light of dawn was just filling the sky, the streets were far from deserted. In the relative cool of early morning people were going about their business. It occurred to her suddenly that the heat no longer bothered her, that she was unaware of when she had ceased to notice it. Of course, said the voice of irony in her mind, she did have other things to think about.

Beside her, Mark squeezed her hand. "I'm glad you've gotten to like the theater we've seen."

His brief chuckle made her turn and look at him. "That first day in my office . . ." He shook his head. "I thought the whole tour would be ruined." He squeezed her hand again. "You sure came on strong."

"I meant every word." And she had. There was no need to tell him that a big part of her irritation that day had had nothing to do with the theater.

"I'm sure you did." His face sobered. "I would never expect you to say anything you didn't mean."

His dark eyes regarded her somberly, but he said no more.

In an effort to lessen the tension between them she asked, "What is your favorite drama?"

Something in his face told her that he knew what she was doing, but all he said was, "I'd have to think. I guess it'd be a toss-up between the Chinese street opera and the *wayang kulit*. Of course, the puppet show only gives the puppeteer a chance to perform. I'm very fond of the *zat pwe*, too. It has some intriguing ramifications. And of course there are many other forms we haven't seen or even talked about. The Cambodians and Vietnamese both have serious musical dramas. And Java has many kinds of theater. Besides the puppet show we saw tonight, there's another without the light and shadows. And a kind of play which has live actors and actresses doing the puppet play stories."

"Like Po Sein used the Jataka stories?"

Mark nodded. "Yes. Also, Java is one of the few Southeast Asian nations to evolve forms without song or dance, done in a realistic style. But song and dance are still a big part of the program, before the play begins and between the acts."

Claudia nodded. "I guess so far I like the Chinese street opera best. It's so colorful."

Mark nodded. "Yes, it is. And very dramatic."

They were at the hotel now and daylight was streaking the sky. She tried not to think beyond the present moment as he held the door for her to pass through. There was no one she knew in the lobby, but when she turned to him her expression was that of a student. "Thank you for staying to the end so that I could see it all."

"You're quite welcome." His tone was formal enough, but his eyes danced with mischief. His voice dropped a tone, so she had to lean forward to hear his words. "It was my pleasure," he continued. "It's not the ordinary way to spend the night with a woman, but at least I was with you."

He didn't wait for her to reply, which was just as well because she could think of nothing to say.

"Better sleep through the morning," he went on.

"Yes." She nodded.

He smiled at her once, and then, his eyes gone suddenly sad, he added, "See you later."

Then he was gone, striding off across the lobby, back out into the city that was coming awake. She made her way to her room and fell into the bed, where, even though she had been up all night, it took her more than an hour to fall asleep.

13

〜ҽҽҽҽҽҽҽҽҽҽ〜

It was around noon when Claudia slowly opened her eyes. Outside her hotel room a city full of people went about its business. But inside, with the sound of the air conditioning as a buffer, she heard nothing.

Still half-asleep, she moved to her right, her hand groping unconsciously for Mark's body. Full awareness came with such suddenness that she drew back her hand as though she'd been burned.

Mark was not there. He would not ever be there when she woke. The thought shuddered through her with a violence that wrenched a dry sob from her depths and made her curl up in a tight little ball.

She'd been dreaming. Hazy tendrils of those feelings still lingered in her consciousness. In the dream they had been in bed, she and Mark. Not in a hotel room, either. She frowned, trying to recapture the details. It had been a nice room—homey, comfortable, familiar. A room she knew and loved, though not any room she had ever seen in reality.

And Mark had been sleeping beside her. Some details she could remember with crystal clarity: The peaceful look on his face as he slumbered there. The way she had leaned to wake him with a kiss. The look of love in his eyes as he opened them. And then, just as he was about to return her kiss, she had wakened—wakened to the reality that Mark was not there, that he would never be there.

The tears crept from beneath her closed eyelids. How good it had felt in that dream to know that she loved Mark and that he returned that love. Another sob made its way from her heart. Now she could see what she had let herself in for. Other women might be able to be with a man and keep their feelings safe. She herself might be able to do it with other men. But she couldn't do it with Mark.

She should have seen that, she told herself bitterly. She should have realized that she loved him. After all these years, she still loved him. She should have seen that and protected herself accordingly.

Well, she told herself, now that she had seen the truth, she'd better face up to it. She might be a slow learner, but this was one lesson she had learned well. She knew what was what now and she would have to make a decision.

There were just a few days left on this trip, but he would probably be expecting to spend at least part of that time with her. The question was, could she handle that? As the tears rolled down her cheeks, she wished desperately that she could just get on a plane and go home. But common sense told her that that wouldn't work. Then she would have to explain to her father.

No, she had to stick it out. Some way or other, she had to get through these remaining days.

The shrill ringing of the phone startled her and she picked it up automatically. "Hello." It was only when she heard his voice that she realized she should have let it ring.

"Hello, Claudia."

"Hel-lo, Mark." Her voice was still thick with tears.

"You sound strange. Is something wrong?"

She said the first thing that came to her mind. "I . . . I was sleeping. The phone woke me."

"Oh, I'm sorry. I thought you'd be awake by now. Are you ready to see Jakarta?"

"I . . ." She couldn't think of an adequate lie.

As though he sensed her reluctance, he hurried on. "Please, Claudia. I need your company today more than ever." She heard the pain in his voice. "This . . . this is where we came on our honeymoon, and . . . it's very difficult for me to be alone."

She longed to respond to the need in his voice, to hold him close and comfort him, but she could find no words.

"I won't make any demands on you," he continued. "Just come with me. Let me show you the sights."

She knew she should tell him no. She had to think of her own feelings. But her love for him ran deep, very deep. And it was no longer tinged with anger. She no longer blamed him for not writing to her. She was able to see how that weekend had seemed to him.

"Please, Claudia."

She was unable to withstand the need in his voice. It touched something deep within her. "All right."

"Great! I'll wait for you in the lobby. Take your time."

She put the phone back in its cradle and sighed. This was probably a big mistake. The sensible thing to do was to avoid him. But then, she told herself grimly as she got to her feet and hurried toward the shower, where Mark was concerned, she seemed to have lost all her sense.

Half an hour later she appeared in the lobby in her off-white pants suit and blue jersey, her clean hair shining.

"You look very rested," Mark said as he rose from a chair to greet her. "Shall we get something to eat first?"

Claudia shrugged. "Whatever you like. I'm not particularly hungry." She was trying to deal with an insane urge to step into his arms, right there in the hotel lobby.

He gave her a rather strange look and, hand on elbow, guided her toward the door.

"Where would you like to go today?" he asked as they reached the street.

"It doesn't matter. You're the one who knows the city."

His fingers had fallen from her elbow as he opened the door for her. She gripped her bag with both hands to keep from reaching out for his.

He stopped there on the street and turned to her. "Claudia, are you sure you're all right?"

"Yes." She'd better pull herself together. "I'm just a little tired." She turned away from his questioning gaze, unwilling to let him look too long at her face. He might see the slight redness around her eyes left by her tears.

His voice was contrite. "I'm sorry. I should have let you sleep. Do you want to go back up to your room?"

"No." The word was spoken before she thought. Painful as it was to be with him, it would be even more painful to go back up to her room and think of him wandering around the city alone. "No, I'll be all right."

"Well, if you're sure." He was still plainly not convinced.

"I'm sure." She managed a small smile. "Let's go somewhere and have some breakfast. Then you can show me Jakarta."

"It's a deal."

With breakfast behind them, Mark took charge. "I think maybe we should just walk around for a while. If the heat's not too much for you."

She shook her head. "I think I'm getting used to it."

"Good. Then we'll just walk and talk. If we can," he added as they stepped from the quiet of the restaurant out into the bustle of the street.

Claudia smiled. "I never thought I'd see any place with worse traffic jams than New York City."

"But now you have."

"Yes. Now I have."

He smiled. "Would you believe it used to be worse?"

She looked out over the crowded street where every variety of car and bus inched along, jammed nose to tail. At the intersection stood a traffic policeman. His arms waving energetically, he alternately cajoled and bullied the mass of traffic into ordered movement. They were close enough to see the whistle in his mouth, but the sound of it was swallowed in the noise of so many motors.

She turned to Mark. "Frankly, I don't see how it could be worse."

"Remember the trishaw we rode in Singapore?"

"Yes." She didn't add that she would remember everything about this trip, probably till the day she died.

"They have a similar thing here—pedicabs or *becaks*, as they're called. They used to be all over the city."

He paused and she saw his jaw tighten as though he were suppressing a wave of pain. "Now the government has been trying to keep them to the suburbs. To help traffic flow more smoothly."

She nodded. Had he been thinking of his wife? Of their honeymoon here? She tried to push the thought from her mind, but it wouldn't go. Probably everything here reminded him of that other woman. Plum Blossom. Claudia envisioned a small, delicate woman with brown almond eyes in a smooth oval face surrounded by glossy black hair.

"If you get too tired," Mark was saying, "or too hot, just holler. This place is built on marshlands, and the humidity can really get to you. Just tell me and we'll find an air-conditioned place for a while. Okay?"

"Okay," she replied, trying to put a cheerful note into her voice and feeling that she had almost succeeded.

As they moved along the crowded sidewalk, she

tried to keep her attention on the city around her. She would probably never be here again. She must make the most of this visit.

"Look over there," Mark said, pulling her out of the flow of pedestrian traffic. "There's a good example of the mingling of East and West."

Claudia looked. A modern office complex, its concrete and glass gleaming in the sun, rose skyward, and right beside it, like something lifted out of a fairy tale, stood an oriental building with terraced roofs shingled in red tile. Following the sweep of Mark's hand, she looked further to where a high-roofed gabled house stood beside another modern building.

"That one's left from Dutch colonial days," Mark said, moving her back into the stream of traffic.

The blast of a horn, sharp even over the traffic noise, made her jump and cling to his arm.

Mark chuckled and put his free hand over hers. "Take it easy. It's just a bus. Look."

Claudia looked, then looked again. To see a bus packed with people wasn't so unusual a sight. Not for a veteran of Cleveland's rush hours. But to see one with people clinging to the outside . . . She could hardly believe her eyes.

"The place is growing so fast," Mark explained, "some services just can't keep up."

They resumed their walk, her hand still through his arm. Along the sidewalks, itinerant merchants had set up little folding tables. Except for an occasional phrase in English, Claudia could not understand what they were saying. But their general intent was clear enough. They were hawking their wares.

One man darted out to offer them an armful of

dangling necklaces. Mark motioned him aside. "They make their living this way," he said. "Sometimes they get a little overly enthusiastic. Let's see. Where shall we go first? Plum Blossom loved the Central Museum. I bet you'd like that."

She stopped herself from wincing as he spoke his late wife's name. It was probably good for him to do so. She was with him today because she loved him, she reminded herself, not because he loved her. If he wanted to talk to a friend about his dead wife, she would be that friend.

"What was she like?" she asked, and then wondered if she had really asked the question for his sake.

He didn't seem to think it odd, though, and as they walked he told her. "She was a tiny little thing. Didn't even come to my shoulder. Looked so fragile. Like she'd break if I touched her."

He smiled wistfully and Claudia felt the knife-sharp edge of pain in her heart. If only he could have loved *her* like that!

"But in spite of her looks she was a fighter. Had to be to live through the war." He frowned. "The things she told me . . . And the things I saw for myself."

He made a gesture of dismissal. "But I won't tell you about that. Just that she was a good person— loving, kind. A good mother."

He paused and she saw him fighting emotion. "The boy was a lot like her," he said finally. "A little fighter. And smart as a whip." He sighed "I had so much," he said softly. "And then suddenly it was all gone. Even the memories were spoiled, so full of pain."

He paused and smiled at her ruefully. "Sorry about that. I didn't mean to get maudlin."

She shook her head. "There's no need to be sorry. It helps sometimes to talk."

He stared at her for a brief moment and she wondered if she had somehow given herself away. "Yes," he said. "It does help. And the pain grows gradually less. I suppose that I'll marry again. Some day."

She turned away quickly, pretending interest in a building to her right while she fought back the tears. She supposed she should make some comment, but the words wouldn't go past the lump in her throat.

"What about you, Claudia? Don't you ever want a husband, a family?"

She had to swallow twice before she could reply. "I have my career." She did not look at him as she spoke. If she had, he might have seen the lie for what it was, might have known what she now needed desperately to hide from him. She didn't have his love, but she certainly didn't want his pity. "My career fills my life." She spoke with a finality that she hoped would discourage him from pursuing the subject. And it did.

The rest of the afternoon passed far too quickly. They visited the Central Museum, where she forced herself to exclaim over a really wonderful collection of the arts and crafts of the various peoples of Indonesia, the ancient stone statues, and the fragile old Chinese ceramics from the Han to the Ming dynasties.

It was not that she didn't appreciate these things. She did. It was only that they seemed to be accompanied by a ghost—the ghost of Plum Blossom.

Downtown, at the old Jakarta Museum, she was able to manage a little better. She could admire its eighteenth-century Dutch architecture and look with interest at the depiction of the development of Jakarta from an East Indies Company trading post to a proud city.

From there they went to the Batik Federation, where she saw the painstaking work that went into the wax and dye process of making the intricately designed material. She watched in awe as one woman drew a design freehand on the cloth, a second sat applying wax to the areas not to be colored, and a third dipped an already prepared piece in the dye pot.

She turned to Mark with admiration showing on her face. "This is really something to see. It must take forever to do, though. All this work by hand."

He nodded. "It takes up to six months sometimes. In the old days, when batiking was an art allowed only to royal women, it was a spiritual as well as an artistic form. A kind of meditation. The designs were all original."

Claudia frowned. "It's sad to think of so many beautiful arts being lost."

Mark squeezed her hand. "For a while, because of a process that made the work much faster, batiking was in danger. But it's making a comeback now. I think people—some people, at least—will always appreciate the beauty of handmade things."

"Yes. I guess you're right. I hope you're right."

They moved back out into the crowded, noisy street, back toward the hotel where the class had earlier decided to have dinner as a group.

As they rounded the corner and the hotel came in view, Mark dropped her hand. She fought a feeling of abandonment so sharp it caught her breath. "Thank you, Claudia. You made the day much easier for me. You're a real friend."

"You're welcome, Mark." She got those words out, but could not think of anything more to say.

He paused. "I guess I'd better let you go into the hotel alone. Goodbye. See you later."

"Goodbye." She stood for a minute, watching until he disappeared into the stream of traffic before she went on into the hotel. It was prophetic, she supposed, this habit of watching him walk away. One day soon he would do it for the last time.

14

~~~~~~~~~~~~~~~~~~~~

The next afternoon she stood at the rail of the ferry watching the beautiful island of Bali draw closer and closer. The land she saw over the glistening blue water looked green and peaceful. The deck of the ferry was not.

Squealing pigs and noisy chickens shared space with great bunches of sweet-smelling flowers and baskets of exotic fruit that Claudia had never seen before. Young men and women wearing the *sarung*, the native dress, stood or sat in small groups around the deck.

Leaning against the rail, Claudia tried to imagine what it would be like to live in this tropical paradise. Imagine having the warm sun and the blue water every day. Imagine wearing a sarung, just a piece of draped cloth. She thought of the length of sari silk tucked carefully away in the bottom of her suitcase. She would probably never wear it, but she was glad to have bought it.

Mark did not come near her on the crossing. Yet in spite of the fact that she knew he was respecting her wishes, she was disappointed. She liked being with him, she explained to herself. Most women would. Surely there was nothing wrong with that. As long as she remembered that nothing was going to come of it. Nothing at all.

Once on the island, she followed the others into the cart for the ride to the village. Mark was in the same cart, but so was Dell, and she stared straight out before her. Unwilling to talk to Dell and unable even to look at Mark, she tried to keep her attention on the lovely countryside. And it was lovely. In all directions the land stretched away, green growing foliage and vari-colored blossoms interspersed with fields of rice plant-ed in neat rows. Over one gently rolling hill she glimpsed the tiered spire of a temple. Along the side of the road, their spines erect, their carriage proud and graceful, walked a single file of supple, sarung-clad young women. But what was most striking about their appearance was the mountains of fruit and flowers balanced so neatly in baskets atop their heads.

"Offerings for the gods," Mark volunteered to those in the cart. "They're probably on their way to the temple. The gods like flowers here."

The cart passed by the line of gracefully swaying young women and Claudia turned to look at them. Their smooth honey-colored faces were strikingly lovely, she thought, wondering what it would be like to live in a country like this, to walk barefoot in a beautiful flowered sarung along a narrow dusty road, on the way to the temple.

With something like shock, she realized that she was envying these young women. From what Mark had told her about Indonesia and Bali, custom reigned supreme. And where that happened a woman's place was known. Life was much simpler in a country like this. There would be no question of a woman living alone here. She would have a man and a family. A woman here could count on that.

Automatically her eyes went to Mark on the other side of the cart, to the face of the only man she had ever wanted to spend her life with. She could not, of course. But she had known that—known it when she first came on this trip. She wrenched her eyes away from him again, but not quite soon enough. His eyes caught at hers. It seemed like he was trying to tell her something, but she couldn't be sure what it was. Then someone next to him tugged on his arm and the moment was gone.

It had been like that the night before. All of them had sat around one large table and Mark had been to her right, in a place where she couldn't easily see him—nor he her. Yet every time she turned her head—and she couldn't stop herself from doing it occasionally—her eyes had met his.

It was so frustrating to be in the same room with the man she loved and to have to pretend he was a stranger. Those two girls who always seemed to be hanging about him got more recognition than she did.

But she had handled her thoughts, she told herself, again focusing on the scene around them. And anyway, last night was over. The sun was shining; the day was beautiful. She pushed away her sad thoughts. She was going to enjoy this day.

After a leisurely ride past rice fields and thatched houses with curved terraced roofs, they reached the village. Half the class climbed down, Claudia among them. "The rest of us will be down the road," Mark told them before the cart moved on. "Get settled in. Remember there's a *kecak* dance performance this evening. We'll attend in a group."

Claudia nodded with the others and, as the cart pulled away, turned to go into her inn. Mark's words had made her think of the night before last. Would they sit up all night again, watching the dance? And even more important, would they be left alone together when it was over?

As she shook out her clothes in the tiny room, which had only a sleeping shelf with a mat rolled up on it and a rod to hang clothes on, she realized that one decision had been spared her. There was no way they could make love here, with the surrounding rooms each inhabited by a class member. The situation would be the same in Mark's inn except that the men, she remembered, all had to sleep in one room. But it would be nice to be left to watch the play together, to sit with his arm around her waist, her head against his shoulder.

Those thoughts were still with her as she joined the others in the courtyard as dusk fell. Several of the girls had bought sarungs and were busy exclaiming over their comfort. It would be fun to be carefree like that; but, she thought ruefully, she was getting too old. In fact, she had only brought the dress she was wearing because it was made of crushable cotton gauze and so wrinkling it didn't matter. She thought of the precious sari, still at the bottom of her bag. She would love to wear it just once, to have Mark see her in it.

He appeared at that moment with the rest of the class and they set off down the road. Mark was in the lead, and she didn't try to move up near him. Knowing that they must behave like teacher and student, she preferred to walk behind. That way she could see his head, the dark hair curling on his collar. Her hands itched to touch it, to touch any part of him. But, of course, she could not.

She moved through the gathering dusk, the dirt of the road gritting beneath her sandals. The heady fragrance of flowers hung in the air. Hibiscus. Jasmine. Bougainvillea. The names had stuck in her head from the guidebook, but she had no way to match them to the actual flowers.

For once, Dell had not come to her side. She could see him slightly ahead of her, making up to one of the women students, and she smiled slightly. Being left more or less to herself didn't bother her at all. She was used to being alone. And if the others didn't stay for the entire performance . . . She didn't allow herself to finish the thought.

They entered a clearing. A space had been set aside as a stage, marked by a semicircle of torches behind it. As they found seats on the ground, a young man with a flaming torch touched each of the embedded ones in turn and they flared into brightness. The sun had set; the performance could begin.

Balinese men, each in a colorful draped sarung, filed in and arranged themselves in rows, making a large semicircle in the area in front of the torches.

Claudia watched with interest. She had read enough in her guidebook to recognize that these were the monkey dancers, members of the army of the monkey king, Hanuman.

She tried counting them as they took their positions, but when she got to one hundred, she gave it up. When they were all seated, the male chorus began chanting. There was no music, no instrument except those powerful voices.

Gooseflesh stood out on Claudia's bare arms as the story progressed. It was a story they had seen before. Rama's wife, Sita, had been abducted by the evil Rhawana. There were dancers to depict these characters and one who portrayed Hanuman, the monkey king. But it was not these actor-dancers, going through their movements in the light cast by the flaring torches, but the monkey chorus that held the attention.

In the gloom of the tree-encircled clearing, with only the torches for light, the seated men *became* monkeys. Their voices, hitting the ear as one sound, moved through the range of human emotion. Compassion, fear, panic, shock, and despair registered on the listeners. In unison the massed bodies swayed, throwing their raised arms to right and left.

And through the night air came moans of sorrow, hisses and bellows of anger, and other unnameable noises that carried such primeval feeling that Claudia began to tremble. She didn't know the language of the play, but this transcended language. She was shaken in the depths of her being.

The performance came finally to an end. The people around her rose and departed. Through the dull murmur of the crowd she was vaguely aware of

Dell's cheerful tones as he passed, still in attendance on the same woman. But Claudia sat on. No dramatic performance in her life had ever moved her so. Bemused, she tried to sort through her emotions. It was not the story; she'd seen it before. There was nothing particularly different about it. There had been no orchestra, so it couldn't have been the music. There had been nothing but those voices, rising as one.

"Claudia."

She looked up in surprise to see Mark standing before her. The area where the audience had been was almost empty, and a young man was going from torch to torch extinguishing them.

"The show's over," Mark said.

"I know." She got slowly to her feet. "I . . . I was thinking about the play."

Mark nodded. His hand on her elbow, he guided her away from the clearing. They hadn't gone far when it occurred to her that they were not going toward her inn. "Isn't my room in the other direction?" she asked, fighting her desire, her need to be with him, which was clamoring to be heeded now that the play was over.

"Yes. But I thought we might walk a little and I didn't think you'd want to be seen with me."

Something in the way he said this made her turn quickly and stare at him. But the shadows hid his face, masking whatever she might have read there. She didn't quite know how to reply, and in a moment they moved on, part of the crowd of homeward bound people.

"It was really a marvelous performance," she said at last, needing the sound of his voice.

"Yes. The *kecak* is one of the most dramatic of all dance-plays."

"I never could have imagined anything like it."

"I'm glad you're becoming fond of the Asian theater," he said. His fingers had slipped from her elbow to enclose her hand, and now he squeezed it.

She laughed a little, remembering again that first day in his office. She had thought of herself as honest and forthright then, but looking back her behavior seemed almost rude. "I guess you wouldn't have suspected it from what I said that first day."

He chuckled. "I'll say. I knew you were carrying a big chip on your shoulder. What really puzzled me was why."

As her cheeks reddened, she was glad for the concealing shadows. The last thing she wanted to discuss was her feelings about this trip. "Where are we going?" she asked, suddenly conscious that the crowd around them had thinned a lot.

"Down the road a little. There's something I want you to see."

"What is it?"

He shook his head. "That would spoil it."

In a few minutes they turned off the road. Under her sandals she felt the soft dust of a narrow path as she followed him. The trees and bushes that were so green in the sunlight gleamed silver-gray in the moonlight. The fragrance of flowers seemed stronger than usual.

They walked for some minutes in silence. There was something about the place, about its eerie beauty, that kept her from speaking. It seemed an enchanted forest, a place where anything could happen.

Finally the path widened. Mark stepped into a little clearing and turned to watch her face as she followed.

She could not stop her quick intake of breath. A little stream meandered slowly along until it widened into a glittering crystal pool. "It's beautiful," she whispered.

"I thought you'd like it. Let's sit down."

He led her toward the edge of the pool. Settling there on the bank of lush green grass, she slipped off her sandals and dangled her feet in the water.

He did the same, slipping his arm around her waist. They sat in silence for some minutes. Then he whispered, his lips close to her ear, "Let's go for a swim."

"I'd love to," she replied, wanting to turn her face so that their lips would touch, but almost afraid to move. "But I haven't any suit."

"Neither have I. But that needn't stop us."

She turned her head quickly. "You're kidding!"

His mouth was very close then and he took advantage of the situation to kiss her. It was a long kiss, and she felt herself growing weak.

When he released her lips, he gestured toward the expanse of shimmering water. "Come on, Claudia," he coaxed. "No one will see us. No one will be coming here this late at night. It's perfectly safe."

He got to his feet with that easy grace she so admired and pulled her after him. Then he began taking off his clothes.

Horrifying visions of discovery raced through her mind, but she also felt a ripple of excitement. Just this once she would like to do something different, something a little dangerous. She made up her mind; she was going to do it. She pulled her dress over her head just as his trousers hit the ground. He waited while she took off the rest of her clothes.

Then he took her hand and, naked together, they stepped into the pool. The water was warm and incredibly sensuous. As it rose around her body, her desire rose too. But what she felt was different somehow. The desire was there, pulsing through her veins, but there was no fevered excitement. Only a languorous, sweet delight.

They turned to each other at the same moment, as though their minds were holding the same thoughts. He put a finger to his lips and she understood. There was a kind of perfect quietness about the little pool and its beauty. It almost seemed as though words might destroy it, make it vanish into the night.

With gestures, he told her to remain standing. The water lapped gently around her waist, like the touch of a lover's hands, she thought, wondering how many Balinese lovers had consummated their love beside this fairy pool.

As she stood there, he gathered the shimmering water in his two cupped hands and anointed each of her breasts, pausing to kiss each rosy peak. In the same way and with the same reverent expression, he poured water over her shoulders and back until she gleamed with moonlit wetness.

When he finished, she did the same for him, liberally anointing his chest and back. In the tree-dappled moonlight their bodies were transformed, became those of fairylike beings.

He reached out his hands to her, drawing her slowly closer until their bodies touched. The languorous delight spread over her. The wetness of their bodies, the strange place, the exotic moonlight, all heightened her responses. She felt herself a primeval woman. The eternal female.

As his lips sought hers, she wrapped her arms around his neck, giving herself fully to his kiss. There was no going back now, no weighing the danger. There was no possible end to this slow ritual meeting of bodies other than their complete union.

They kissed for many minutes, their bodies entwined there in the silver water. She felt delight spreading and growing, swallowing her so completely that nothing else mattered.

Finally he released her lips and led her slowly back to the grassy bank. She needed no gesture to indicate his intent. They sank down together on the lush grass, their bodies still entwined.

It seemed to Claudia that time had slowed. Each kiss, each caress, lasted long, lovely minutes. When finally he joined them, she felt no urgency, only that sweet delight.

He seemed to be affected in the same way. He moved against her slowly and gently, and her delight grew and grew until she heard the brief exclamation that marked his release and she dissolved into a pool of sweet contentment.

It was really like that, she mused, as, lying there against him, she began to think again. She had felt dissolved. And yet she had not felt less. In fact, she had felt more. Part of something bigger than herself. She could hardly put words to it. The universe, perhaps?

Her thoughts roamed as her body snuggled closer against his. Maybe that was what had happened to her at the monkey dance. She had been caught up in something bigger than herself. But there was more to this than what had happened in the clearing. For a while, for those few brief moments, she had felt utterly and completely at peace. With Mark, with herself, with the whole world.

It was because she loved him, she told herself. Her love had made the experience almost mystical.

The pain came so suddenly, so sharply, that it was all she could do to keep from crying out. Loving him in this way was apt to destroy her. She had loved him once, twelve long years ago. And that love had ruined her life, kept her from experiencing this joy, this wonder again.

Lying there in the moonlight, her body against his, she made her decision. She had done all she could for Mark. She had helped him reenter life. She had been his friend.

But friendship didn't mean the destruction of self. And that was clearly the way she was headed if she slept with Mark again. She had to withdraw from him now for her own safety. Because if she didn't, she wouldn't be able to do what she knew must be done.

She had let her love for Mark poison her, let it keep her from experiencing love with anyone else. She didn't want to do that anymore. She had been wrong to close herself off as she had. Back in Cleveland, with Mark safely gone, she was going to build a new life for herself. It would have to be without him, but it wouldn't have to be without love.

15

Late the next evening Claudia stood by the railing of the Chinese junk *Fairwind*, looking out over the harbor of Singapore. The flight back from Bali had been uneventful. She had not seen Mark alone since he'd left her outside the door of her inn the night before.

She pushed that thought from her mind and her hands went unconsciously to smooth the silken sari over her hips. In the morning they would leave for Cleveland. This cruise had been her last chance to wear it. Dell's raised eyebrows had not helped her shyness much, but his later compliment had been sincere.

The lights of the city sparkled in the distance as the junk moved slowly back toward it. Her memories of the evening were already hazy, blurred by the tension of wearing her new gown and the knowledge of her decision.

More than once during the slow cruise she had felt Mark's eyes on her. At the buffet he had been right behind her in the line, so close that several times he had brushed against her. Under the silken sari her body quivered at the remembrance. Once he had whispered, "You look lovely," and she had needed all her strength not to turn and kiss him.

But now the buffet was over. Mark was inside dancing with each of the women in the class. She had come out, into the cool breeze, to get away. To avoid his asking her. Being in his arms might make her give herself away. She was better off out here.

"Claudia."

She turned to Dell, realizing in that instant that she had been hoping for Mark to come to her.

"Hi." Dell leaned on the railing beside her, his shoulder brushing hers. "You're really looking great tonight," he said, turning slowly toward her.

She turned too. "Thank you. I thought I might as well wear this once."

He nodded, his eyes changing.

She saw it coming, read his intent clearly, as over his shoulder she caught a glimpse of Mark. She took the step that brought her into Dell's arms and raised her mouth for his kiss.

When she opened her eyes, Mark was no longer there and Dell was looking rather startled. "The moonlight," she said, half in explanation, half in apology.

"Of course. I understand."

She hoped he didn't, not really; but when he

wanted to take her back inside to dance, she went. The music was quite nice and the atmosphere very romantic, but all she could think of was that look of surprise on Mark's face when he saw her in Dell's arms. She had closed her eyes right away. But not soon enough. Not soon enough to avoid seeing the look of hurt that had followed.

As they returned to a table, she tried to focus her thoughts on something else, to keep her face smooth and cheerful. She certainly didn't want anyone to know that she was upset.

"Miss Carstairs."

His voice sent shivers down her spine. She forced herself to turn and look at him.

"May I have this dance?"

She pushed herself to her feet. To refuse him would be to court all kinds of speculation. She let him lead her to the dance floor, let him put his arm around her. His touch sent her body racing with tremors of desire, but he didn't pull her close against him as she half hoped he would. He held her stiffly.

It was like dancing with a complete stranger. As they circled the dance floor in utter silence, she knew that she had wounded him deeply. She longed to comfort him, to hold him close and ease his pain. But she said nothing. He was feeling rejected and she was sorry. But she had to protect herself.

From the way he was holding her now, certainly no one would ever suspect that there had been anything between them. She forced a smile to her numb lips, hugging to herself the bitter knowledge that if what had passed between them had meant something to him, if it had had any future, she would have been the first to shout it from the housetops.

Their dance ended and she accepted the offers of the other male members of the class. She even managed to laugh and smile with apparent enjoyment. But actually she wanted nothing more than for the cruise to be over, for the whole tour to be over. Her need for him was suffocating her. It was torture to be so close to him, to be so close and yet unable to reach out and touch him. And even worse to have him behave toward her this way.

She knew that her decision had been the right one. Every time they came together her love for him had expanded, filled her whole being. And that wasn't good at all. She had to forget him—to forget him as soon as possible. And the best way to do that was to keep away from him.

The *Fairwind* returned to the harbor. Claudia, her heart aching behind her false smiles and laughter, finally reached the security of her hotel room. With tears in her eyes, she slowly unwound the beautiful sari. Why hadn't she worn it before, some time when she had been with Mark? She folded it carefully, tucking the paper of instructions inside, and returned it to its tissue paper safety in the bottom of her bag.

Shrugging into her short robe, she tried to calm herself. The worst was over now. Mark wouldn't come around her anymore, not after what he had seen tonight.

She threw herself across the bed and tried to relax. She had made the right decision. She was sure she had.

A sharp rap at the door brought her quickly to her feet. Who could be there now? "Just a minute." She tugged her robe tight and went to open the door. "Mark!"

He didn't wait for an invitation, but brushed her aside and slammed the door behind him. Her heart was pounding and her palms were wet, but she kept reminding herself of her decision, of its rightness.

He stood there, hands on hips, glaring at her. She had never seen him angry like this. "What . . . what do you want?"

"I want some answers," he said, his voice like a knife. "And they better be good ones."

"I don't know what you're talking about."

His eyes grew darker with anger. "The hell you don't. First you say stupid things about marriage. Then you quit seeing me. And *then* you start making out with that pitiful excuse for a man!"

"What I do is my business!" she replied hotly. "And exactly what stupid thing did I say about marriage?"

"You told me you were busy with your career. That it filled your life. The more I think about that the dumber I think it is. I thought you were liberated." His handsome face twisted into a sneer. "No man would say a dumb fool thing like that.

"If you're afraid to live, afraid to love, then at least be honest about it. Admit that you're a coward, hiding out in the ivory tower."

"I'm not afraid," she began, but faltered to a stop as he continued to glare at her.

"Love, real love, means commitment. In my book that means marriage." He took a step toward her, then turned suddenly away, his voice choking. "I was so happy. I thought I'd found someone to share my life with again. Someone I love madly and who also has a brain."

He whirled to face her, swiping angrily at the wetness on his cheeks. "But the way you've been acting lately, I'm not sure you have a brain."

She thought her pounding heart would suffocate her. "Did you . . ." She had to force the words past the lump in her throat. "Did you say someone you love?"

"Of course that's what I said. Do you think I make a habit of sleeping with my students?"

"I have no way of knowing," she replied, stung by his harsh tone. "You never mentioned love to me. You talked about Plum . . . about your dead wife."

"How could I mention love?" he demanded. "You'd just told me you had no use for marriage. Told me quite definitely."

He pounded one fist into the other. "I couldn't believe you were still unmarried after all these years. I thought of you so often after our weekend. I imagined you with the others. I wondered if you'd remember me."

The laughter that broke from her then was almost hysterical. "Oh, I remembered you, all right. You were my first. I waited and waited, but you never wrote." She was close to tears, but she wasn't going to give in to them. Let everything come out now.

"Your first? You waited?" He stared at her. "But you didn't tell me. I thought I was just another soldier on leave. I didn't think I was important to you. I told myself it wasn't fair to write and ask you to wait for me when you were so young and carefree."

"Carefree? Her voice had reached a hysterical pitch. "Carefree? I've loved you all these long years, suffered over you, and now you want the chance to hurt me again. How can I believe you?" This was all happening too fast. She shouldn't be telling him all this.

He crossed the distance between them. He was still angry. His chest heaved beneath his shirt. He grabbed her and shook her lightly. "Of course you can believe me. Risk a little. So what if your much-loved Shakespeare warns against giving hostages to fate. You have to be willing to love, to taste joy. And, yes, to risk the loss of your love, and the pain that follows. That's what living's all about, Claudia. Risk is the name of the game."

She shook her head. "I . . . It's all so fast."

He pulled her against him and kissed her savagely, almost crushing her. Yet she was not afraid. How could she be afraid, she realized suddenly, as long as she could be with the man she loved? It was risky; of course it was risky. But Mark was right. Living itself was risky. But not being with him . . . She saw clearly how bleak such a future appeared.

When he released her mouth, he held her off a little, his eyes searching her face. "Say it, Claudia," he begged. "Say you love me."

"I told you that already."

"Say it again. I love the sound of it."

There was joy in his voice now. She could hear it. "I love you."

"Great. That's great. Now when can we get married?"

Laughter bubbled out of her. This was real. It was like a dream but it was really happening. "I have to finish my dissertation."

He grinned. "I don't believe anyone has ever proved that unmarried people write better dissertations. Besides"—he kissed the tip of her nose—"I type sixty words a minute and my services come with the job."

She laughed again and hugged him to her. "You've made me an offer I can't resist. But seriously, Mark, I can't very well leave Cleveland until it's finished."

"Well then, I guess I'll have to wait—to marry you, that is. How long do you think it'll take?"

Her grin matched his. "The research is almost all done. Say, three or four months."

"Say three or less," he urged. "After all, I'm only human. Let's set the date now. How about Thanksgiving? That's a good day to begin a new life. I'll be doubly grateful."

"Me, too." She buried her face in his throat.

"So." His hands crept up under her short robe. "You've promised to marry me on Thanksgiving?"

"Yes."

"Well, I'm willing to wait for marriage, but I'm not willing to wait for love. Here we are, all alone in this hotel room, and there's a bed right over there. What else can we ask for?"

"Nothing," she replied, reaching for the buttons on his shirt. "Nothing at all."

YOU'LL BE SWEPT AWAY WITH SILHOUETTE DESIRE

$1.75 each

1 ☐ James	5 ☐ Baker	8 ☐ Dee
2 ☐ Monet	6 ☐ Mallory	9 ☐ Simms
3 ☐ Clay	7 ☐ St. Claire	10 ☐ Smith
4 ☐ Carey		

$1.95 each

11 ☐ James	29 ☐ Michelle	47 ☐ Michelle	65 ☐ Allison
12 ☐ Palmer	30 ☐ Lind	48 ☐ Powers	66 ☐ Langtry
13 ☐ Wallace	31 ☐ James	49 ☐ James	67 ☐ James
14 ☐ Valley	32 ☐ Clay	50 ☐ Palmer	68 ☐ Browning
15 ☐ Vernon	33 ☐ Powers	51 ☐ Lind	69 ☐ Carey
16 ☐ Major	34 ☐ Milan	52 ☐ Morgan	70 ☐ Victor
17 ☐ Simms	35 ☐ Major	53 ☐ Joyce	71 ☐ Joyce
18 ☐ Ross	36 ☐ Summers	54 ☐ Fulford	72 ☐ Hart
19 ☐ James	37 ☐ James	55 ☐ James	73 ☐ St. Clair
20 ☐ Allison	38 ☐ Douglass	56 ☐ Douglass	74 ☐ Douglass
21 ☐ Baker	39 ☐ Monet	57 ☐ Michelle	75 ☐ McKenna
22 ☐ Durant	40 ☐ Mallory	58 ☐ Mallory	76 ☐ Michelle
23 ☐ Sunshine	41 ☐ St. Claire	59 ☐ Powers	77 ☐ Lowell
24 ☐ Baxter	42 ☐ Stewart	60 ☐ Dennis	78 ☐ Barber
25 ☐ James	43 ☐ Simms	61 ☐ Simms	79 ☐ Simms
26 ☐ Palmer	44 ☐ West	62 ☐ Monet	80 ☐ Palmer
27 ☐ Conrad	45 ☐ Clay	63 ☐ Dee	81 ☐ Kennedy
28 ☐ Lovan	46 ☐ Chance	64 ☐ Milan	82 ☐ Clay

YOU'LL BE SWEPT AWAY WITH SILHOUETTE DESIRE

$1.95 each

83 [ ] Chance	93 [ ] Berk	103 [ ] James	113] Cresswell
84 [ ] Powers	94 [ ] Robbins	104]Chase	114 [ ] Ross
85 [ ] James	95 [ ] Summers	105]Blair	115 [ ] James
86 [ ] Malek	96 [ ] Milan	106]Michelle	116 [ ] Joyce
87 [ ] Michelle	97 [ ] James	107]Chance	117 [ ] Powers
88 [ ] Trevor	98 [ ] Joyce	108]Gladstone	118 [ ] Milan
89 [ ] Ross	99 [ ] Major	109 [ ] Simms	119 [ ] John
90 [ ] Roszel	100 [ ] Howard	110 [ ] Palmer	120 [ ] Clay
91 [ ] Browning	101 [ ] Morgan	111 [ ] Browning	
92 [ ] Carey	102 [ ] Palmer	112 [ ] Nicole	

Coming Next Month

Late Rising Moon by Dixie Browning

Larain expected to get control of her life again as manager of Silas Flynt's art gallery. Instead the icy facade she cultivated melted completely as she abandoned herself in Silas' arms.

Without Regrets by Brenda Trent

Despite their vow never to part, Halette and Kale's blissful marriage had shattered. Now, amidst the splendors of the Orient, the old passions flared again, strong and steady, and challenged all their hesitations.

Gypsy Enchantment by Laurie Paige

Keri Thomas had left Louisiana and Reid Beausan to begin her life again in Houston. But on her return, the man who had stolen her innocence seduced her again, rekindling passions she had been desperate to forget.

Color My Dreams by Edith St. George

When cool Robyn Stuart travelled to Fiji to lure artist Philip Holt back to civilization, she didn't expect to be seduced by the primitive pulse of the island—and discover her own primitive passions in the arms of its devastating inhabitant.

Passionate Awakening by Gina Caimi

Arden knew it was a chance in a lifetime when she was commissioned to write the biography of reclusive tycoon Flint Masters. But her objectivity gave way once Flint revealed his most private self to her—and his sudden interest in her as a woman.

Leave Me Never by Suzanne Carey

It was an honor to be accepted as a student under the great Dr. Benjamin Reno. But Terry had to fight her feelings for the man who had claimed her body and soul six years before—and whose eyes now burned with anger as well as passion.